Legacy of the Undead

My Life Among the Undead:

Book 8

Camara M. Bragdon

For more information, or to book an event, contact :
www.camarambragdonauthor.com

Book design by Camara M. Bragdon
Cover design by Camara M. Bragdon

ISBN - 978-1-964265-07-0

My Life among the Undead Books

By

Camara M. Bragdon

Friend of the Undead

Yard Sale of the Undead

Secrets of the Undead

Carnival of the Undead

Holiday of the Undead

Reunion of the Undead

Election of the Undead

DEDICATION

This book is dedicated to all my sisters, Bethany, Leanne, Becky, Melanie, and Beulah. Thanks for being such awesome sisters!

CHAPTERS

Prologue

I was alone in the Lapis Lazuli Room of the city of Zephyr Community Center as I prepped for my seven o'clock wedding. Last night, my fiance, Eddie Van Helsing, and I had separated the one hundred silver plastic chairs in two separate groups on each side of the rooms. By the time we were done, we had five rows consisting of tens on both sides with a gap wide enough for the bridal party to walk to the elevated stage. Each row was decorated with metallic blue roses with deep purple ribbons hanging from the sides of the end chairs. The stage had been decorated similarly as the white lattice arch combined the roses, fabrics, and twinkle lights, making the blue room absolutely gorgeous. Hey, I was getting married at night, so why not? This room was set for tonight. Now for the reception room.

Eddie and I had chosen the Amethyst Room, not only because it was inexpensive but also the light purple color scheme. Ten round tables were adorned with metallic blue linen tablecloths with ten purple plastic place settings each. The sweetheart table near the front had a purple tablecloth and two metallic blue place settings. Everything was in order. I breathed a huge sigh of relief as I placed my hands on my hips.

The door opened, and my best friend and maid of honor, Lisa Miller, rushed into the room. A horrified look appeared in her bright green eyes. "Shelly Anderson!"

"What?" I asked.

"You're getting married in two hours, and your makeup's not even done."

I sighed. "I don't need tons of makeup plastered on my face, Lisa."

"Don't you wanted to look beautiful for your wedding pictures?" she asked.

"We agreed on just lipstick," I reminded her as we walked to the Jade Room, where my stepmother and the other bridesmaids were getting ready for the ceremony. The light green room only had four tables and a few chairs. The community center had even loaned us two privacy screens on wheels.

"Oh, Shelly, there you are," my stepmother said. The beautiful woman in her fifties gave me a big hug.

"I was just making sure the rooms were ready."

Amelia Anderson's hazel eyes smiled at me. "Are you nervous?"

"A little," I admitted. "I just want the day to go smoothly."

"It will. Don't worry. Oh, by the way, someone dropped off an envelope for you. Cricket put it by your purse."

I walked over to the table where my dress, shoes, purse, and accessories lay. I opened a strange white envelope. Hastily written across the single sheet of copy paper were the words: Too many people here. Enjoy your day. No signature.

I glanced around the room. My stepmother, Lisa, and my other three bridesmaids were the only other people here. "Do you guys know who dropped this off?"

Cricket Lunesta fluttered her pale, green wings as she flew over to me. "Sorry, someone left it by the door."

I shrugged it off. "Weird." I pushed the mysterious letter to the back of my mind and focused on the task ahead. "Alright," I said, pointing to my shoulder-length brown hair, "Let's get ready."

I watched the last two members of the bridal party walk down the aisle from the hall. Standing off the right of the decorated arch was my dashing husband-to-be with his groomsmen. The purple and blue paper pinwheel bouquet shook in my hands.

"I wish Mom could see how beautiful you look today," my dad, Timothy Anderson, said as he linked his arm with mine. He looked at me with his baby blue eyes.

"Me too," I replied with a sigh. It had been over fifteen years since my mother had passed away. Even though I loved my stepmother, I still wished my mother could be with me on my wedding day.

"When Mom and I got married," Dad said, "I was so nervous until I saw her walking down the aisle. I knew that whatever happened that day didn't matter to me because I was marrying the love of my life."

"Thanks, Dad. That does help." I locked eyes with my husband-to-be in the other room and smiled. Instantly my nerves melted away. The rest of that beautiful night was the best time I had ever had.

Six months later

I checked my watch as I waited for my husband to pick me up. It was almost three in the morning. It was pitch black on the empty street, save the lonely, flickering street light. "Eddie, where are you?" I asked as I stood outside the Zephyr Public Library, where I had just finished the graveyard shift. I reached into my light blue leather purse and pulled out my cell phone.

I looked around before calling a very familiar number. It went directly to voicemail, meaning he was still at the diner. "Hey, this is Eddie Van Helsing," my husband's recorded voice said. "Sorry, I can't come to the phone right now, but if you leave your name and number, I'll get back to you as soon as I can."

"Eddie, it's Shelly. It's almost three, and you were supposed to pick me up an hour ago. You're probably still tied up at the diner. I'm going to walk home. Don't forget we have to pick up a gift for Bruce and Libby's wedding. I was thinking about a gift card. Anyway, I'll see you at home. Love you." I hung up the phone and started walking home.

I rubbed my tired eyes. I still wasn't used to a vampire's sleeping schedule. Yes, I'm married to a vampire. A non-brooding, sexy vampire with gorgeous green eyes and short, curly hair that's black as midnight.

I'm not a vampire yet. I'm just your average telepathic human librarian who has lived in Zephyr for about seven years. You can't find the city on any ordinary map, but then again, it's not your everyday city. In fact, Zephyr's in another reality altogether.

It's where myth and magic walk side by side, and casting spells are an everyday occurrence. I came here through a wormhole through space and time, along with my father and brother. My childhood was completely normal. Magic and vampires were only found in books and films. Imagine my shock when my family arrived here. Not only did we discover vampires, fairies, satyrs, and many other mythological creatures really did exist, but we also had acquired a superpower. Mine? The ability to read and communicate with the dead and undead on a mental level, aka telepathy. One would think this would hurt our marriage, but Eddie was the only one who actually helped me understand and control my telepathy. That was years before we started dating.

In a couple of weeks, I was about to take my next lifetime commitment: turning into a vampire via blood transfusion. Believe me, it's less messy and a whole lot safer than the old school way. Transforming someone into a vampire through biting is highly illegal because the bite will paralyze the person, rendering him or her completely helpless. Because of this, it's also illegal to turn someone if he or she is under eighteen.

My sister-in-law had gone through the blood transfusion process about two months ago with Eddie's vampire brother and was doing great. I, on the other hand, was a little nervous about the whole procedure. Not a big fan of needles, especially when the nurse can't find your vein.

I was so lost in my own thoughts that I didn't notice the man in front of me until he drove a piston-powered foot into my chest, throwing me to the ground. I heard the back of my skull crack open the moment I hit the pavement. I let out a horrified scream. Please, someone, help me! I tried to take a breath, but incredibly sharp pains radiated up and down my entire body. My head racked with excruciating pain, and my vision started blurring. Fight, Shelly, I told myself. You've got to fight!

I glanced up at my attacker, intent on remembering every detail if I survived. He was a tall vampire, over six-feet tall, with long, bone-white hair pulled back in a ratty ponytail. He was dressed entirely in black and wore a dark overcoat. But his eyes, I will never forget them. He looked down at me with evil, yellow eyes flecked with red. I tried to gouge out those vile eyes, but he caught my hand in a vise-like grip and slammed it onto the ground.

"You're a fighter," he snarled. "I like it when they fight."

I tried to scream again, but the moment I inhaled, I felt a sharp, stabbing pain rushed to my chest. He straddled me and ripped at my collar. A horrifying realization swept through me as I read his mind: He was about to drink all of my blood.

"This is for the queen," he hissed into my ear. He began tearing at my throat like a rabid dog, his fangs sinking deeper and deeper into my skin with each painful bite. Blood, my blood, sprayed all around us. I was dying, and there was nothing I could do.

Suddenly, a blinding light flashed before us. My attacker hissed and shrank back in terror. He jumped off me and ran. Then my world faded into complete and utter darkness.

When I woke up, I felt someone holding my hand. As I opened my bleary eyes, I saw a reassuring figure leaning forward in an overstuffed chair near my hospital bed. "Eddie?" I whispered hoarsely.

My husband looked up at me, his green eyes red from crying. "Oh, God, Shelly! You're awake!" he said, choking on every word. He threw his arms around me as he kissed me. I tried to swallow, but my throat ached. I decided to use my telepathy. *It hurts to talk*, I mentally told my husband. Tears filled my blue eyes.

You'll heal, babe, he told me as he brushed back my shoulder-length, brown hair from my face.

Did they catch him?

Eddie shook his head. "No, he was gone by the time help arrived." He clenched his fists as his eyes flashed with anger. "But I will find him, and when I do, he will regret the day he was born."

What happened to me?

Eddie hesitated. "You died, but. . ." his voice trailed off.

I glanced over at the heart monitor and noticed how slow it was. I began to hyperventilate. *What's wrong with the monitor? Get the nurse! Get the nurse!* I mentally screamed at Eddie.

"Calm down, Shell. It's going to be alright," he said as he stroked my hand.

In my panic, I ran my tongue over one of my sharp canines. The coppery taste of blood filled my mouth. I knew that I would become one eventually, but not like this. "Oh, God, Eddie!" I said hoarsely, as I began to sob. "He turned me into a vampire!"

Chapter One:
Strange Dreams and Vaguely Familiar Faces

"Mrs. Van Helsing?"

I turned away from the three-ring binder of mug shots to face the young elfin uniformed police officer. "Yes?"

"Which one attacked you?" he asked.

Panic overwhelmed me as I tried to focus on the vampires in the album. None of them even closely resembled my attacker. Was he hiding in the pages, staring up at me with his yellow eyes? My whole body began to shake with fear as I touched the bandage around my almost healed neck.

Eddie put a protective arm around me. "You all right, Shell?" he asked quietly.

I shook my head. "I want to go home, Eddie."

"Do you recognize any of these men, Mrs. Van Helsing?" the officer asked me again.

"No," I replied.

"Detective Anderson mentioned you can read vampires' minds, and he said you might have gotten some information from your attacker."

"The only information I got from him was the fact he was killing me!" I snapped angrily at the elf.

Eddie stared him down with piercing green eyes. "Are we done here?" he asked in a very irritated voice.

The police officer hesitated before he spoke. "This is Detective Anderson's case, and I don't think that would be a good idea."

"Well, let me go talk to him," Eddie said as he got up from the table. "Where is he?"

The interview room door opened, and my brother stepped in. "We can talk right here, Eddie," he said.

"What is your problem, Robin?" my husband demanded. "I told you Shelly wasn't up to answering questions! She just got out of the hospital!"

"I don't want the case to go cold." My brother looked past Eddie and straight at me with his deep blue eyes. "So, was he in there, Shelly?”

“No.”

“Are you sure about your description of him?”

“Yes,” I replied. “The guy had bone-white hair and yellow eyes!”

My brother raised a skeptical eyebrow. “Are you sure his eyes were yellow?”

“I’m positive! Why do you doubt me?”

“Because the description you gave matched no one in our databases!”

“Did you try all the databases?” I demanded of my brother.

“Shelly, trauma victims—,” Robin started to say, but I cut him off.

“Well, couldn’t you run a DNA match on his blood or saliva? I’m sure he left plenty of it on me during the attack!” I shouted as I began to move swiftly toward Robin.

My husband moved quickly between us. “Enough, both of you!” he ordered. We stopped arguing and looked at Eddie. “Robin, my wife and I would like to leave now.” The tone in his voice was not unlike a military commander, and there was no room for argument.

Robin threw up his hands in disgust. "Fine!" he snapped. "Go! I'll let you know if anything develops," he said to Eddie, but not to me.

Eddie took my arm and quickly led me out of the police station where his orange, carrot-shaped car was waiting in the parking lot. He reached in his jeans pocket, pulled out the keys, and unlocked the vehicle remotely. He walked me to the passenger side and opened the door for me.

"Thanks, hon," I mumbled as I slid inside. After I buckled in, I leaned forward and cupped my head in my hands.

Eddie got into the driver's seat and was about to start the engine. "Babe," was all he said as he pulled me to him.

Tears started to fill my eyes as I fought hard to choke back the sobs. Finally, I just gave in and buried my face into his shirt. He said nothing but gently stroked my hair.

When we got home, I noticed something had changed around the five houses that served as our little community. "Eddie?" I asked.

"Yeah, Shelly?" he asked as he unlocked the front door.

I set the six-pack of vile swamp rat blood that the hospital gives new vampires, on the ground and placed my hands on my hips as I surveyed the five little flowerbeds. Our former satyr landlord, Simon Boer, had installed twelve, four-foot-tall, old-fashioned lamp posts among the various flowers. I walked over to the nearest garden and inspected the plants. "They're all withered," I whispered in surprise.

Eddie came over to me. "Is everything all right?"

My fingers barely brushed over a red tulip petal, and it crumbled to pieces. "Something's wrong with the flowers."

"We'll tell the pixies in the morning."

Maybe it was my imagination or my new heightened vampire senses, but I could smell a faint chemical scent all around us. "Insecticides!"

Eddie's brow furrowed in thought. "Are you sure?"

I nodded as I picked up a handful of dry dirt. "There seems to be no water or nutrients in the soil."

He knelt down next to me and combed through the soil with his fingers. "You're right, but the pixies are supposed to be taking care of the flowers. There's no need for insecticides. It's toxic to pixies!"

I pushed back a tangle of weeds to reveal a smashed up pixie home. Tiny furniture was scattered across the dirt. "Raine!" I shouted. "Addison!" Silence echoed all around us. My mind raced to one horrible, ugly conclusion: the pesticide had killed the pixie family. Righteous anger and grief-filled my emotions. "How could he do this to them, Eddie? I'm going to give Vinnie a piece of my mind!"

"Shelly," Eddie reminded me, "it's three o'clock in the morning. He's probably sleeping or passed out somewhere."

My hands shook with anger as I pushed Eddie away. "No! I'm going to talk to him right now, and then I'm going to have him arrested for murder!"

"Shell—," Eddie started to say, but I cut him off.

"He's a cold-blooded killer, just like the vampire who turned me!" I nearly shouted at him as tears blurred my vision. I sank to the ground and cupped my head in my hands. *Don't cry, Shelly,* I told myself.

Eddie put his hand on my shoulder and helped me to my feet. "Shelly, let's go inside," he said softly.

"Okay." I picked up the bottles of blood and went into the house. I became depressed all over again the moment I saw my book, which changes into a sword with just a magical phrase and my shield bracelet. On the day I was attacked, I left them sitting on the table, telling myself not to bother bringing them with me. "They're just an added weight," I had told myself. "Plus, what are the chances I would need them?" How could I have been so stupid? What was I thinking? I swallowed the huge lump in my throat.

Eddie took the bottles from me and put them in the refrigerator. "Shell, what do you want for dinner?"

I shrugged. "Whatever." I trudged off to the spare bedroom, which we had converted into my art studio and shut the door. Drawing is one of the few things I can throw myself into and forget the world around me. Boy, did I need that right now! I grabbed a charcoal pencil on a nearby table and began to sketch furiously on my easel. Five minutes and twenty crumpled up pages later, I put down the writing utensil and stared at the blank canvas. The only image replaying in my mind was the face of my attacker. As hard as I tried, I couldn't erase it from my mind.

I gave up drawing and went out into the kitchen. Eddie was staring at our dwindling food supply in the refrigerator. "Is frozen pizza all right with you, babe?" he asked.

I gave a noncommittal shrug as I picked up my book/magic sword and shield bracelet. "Sure. I'll be up in the loft," I told him.

Once I was upstairs, I snapped on my bracelet decorated with a blue lion surrounded by three fleurs-de-lis and pressed the little button on its underside. Immediately, a round shield made from impervious metal fanned out from the bracelet. One weapon ready, one more to go. I touched the pocket-size book that I had placed on the floor and softly said the incantation, "Knowledge is Power." Green sparks swirled around the red leather-bound book as it magically turned into a sixteen-inch blade of pure unbreakable silver. I picked it up and began furiously fighting an invisible enemy. "I won't let you attack me again!" I shouted as my sword cut through the air. I parried back and forth, lifting up my shield to fend off my invisible attacker. "Take that, and that!"

"Shelly, what are you doing?" Eddie asked me. I didn't

even hear him coming up the stairs. I whirled around and nearly

impaled him with a jab of my sword.

I gasped in horror with what I had almost done.

Knowledge clattered to the floor as I deactivated my shield.

"Eddie, I-I'm sorry," I stammered. "I thought you were him, and I

was trying—."

He gave me a tight hug. "It's okay, Shell. No harm done."

"No, it's not!"

"What do you mean?"

"What do you think I mean!" I snapped angrily as I broke

free from my husband. "Look what he did to me!"

"But you were already planning on becoming a vampire by

a blood transfusion."

Tears filled my eyes. "I know, but getting attacked wasn't

my idea!"

He sighed, not quite knowing the right words to say.

Instead, he put his arms around me and said, "Let's have supper

and go to bed."

I nodded slowly as I picked up my sword and said,

"Without Knowledge, there is no power." The weapon turned

back into a harmless book, which I slipped into my pants pocket. "You're right, honey. I just need a good night's sleep to clear my head." But my heart didn't believe what my lips were saying.

We walked down to the kitchen where my husband had set the table with two hot, steaming pieces of four-cheese pizza on our plates. He had even poured me a half-glass of the swamp rat blood. I managed a little smile at him. We sat down, and I took a tentative sip of the blood. I shuddered in revulsion as the liquid slid down my throat. "Still tastes vile every time I try it." I set the glass down and took a bite out of my pizza. "Before you found out about your blood allergy, what kinds of blood did you like the best?"

Eddie thought about it for a moment. "I only tried two kinds. Pig's blood wasn't too bad, but it tasted like bacon. Sheep's blood was okay and had an oat-like taste." Both he and his brother, Dirk, have a rare genetic disorder that makes them highly allergic to blood. My poor husband can't even keep down one sip of blood and hasn't eaten a piece of meat since he became a vampire over forty-years ago. Suddenly, he opened his mouth but hesitated.

"Eddie, were you going to say something?" I asked.

"No!" he lied.

I tried to read his mind, but he purposely blocked me. I tried not to show my surprise because Eddie rarely closed off my telepathy. "Is everything okay?" I asked.

"Yeah, I'm just glad to have you home safe." He avoided the subject, but I was too tired to argue. "Maybe David's book could give you pointers on kinds of blood." Our friend, the wizard David Endora, had just published a book for new vampires and their families called Vampirism for Dummies. Instead of the standard yellow and black cover, the book was decked out in red and black with a Dummies' version of a vampire waving up at the reader.

I shrugged. "I'll look at it later," I replied before wearily finishing off my pizza. An upside to being a vampire, I could still eat all the foods I liked. Eddie and I both looked up from our supper when we heard a loud commotion coming from our postcard-size backyard. "What in the world is going on out there?" I asked as I pushed my chair back from the table.

Eddie followed me to our living room, where I pulled back

the light-blocking curtain from the sliding door. Our new landlord, Vinnie Boer, was too cheap to install UV-protected windows when Eddie moved in with me, and so we had to make do with substandard light-blocking window treatments. "Oh, my God, Eddie! Quentin's in trouble!"

A golden-headed griffin was attempting to fly away from a three-headed hellhound, but one of his eight-foot-long, golden wings was bent at an awkward angle. He turned around and swatted at the hellhound with one of his two front talons. His tail on his tawny lion's hind end swished back and forth in a terrified panic. He looked at us. "Help!" he shouted.

I slid open the door. "In here, Quentin!"

Quentin sprinted inside with the vicious hellhound on his heels. "Close the door! Close the door!" the griffin screamed at me.

"I got it," Eddie said. He slid the door shut and locked it just as the griffin's attacker slammed into the glass, barking loud enough to cause a chain reaction of our nearby neighbors' lights to turn on as they shouted obscenities at both animals. The hellhound cried nonstop for a few more minutes before retreating to her own backyard.

Hellhounds are a real piece of work. They are a tad smaller than a Shetland pony, have three heads with sharp teeth which would make a vampire jealous, and are more aggressive than a swarm of angry wasps. Then again, what do you expect from a dog whose ancestors guarded the gates of Hades? About fifty years ago, some moron had the brilliant idea of crossbreeding hellhounds with regular dogs, and now you have hellhounds with vicious dog blood running through their veins. Poopsie was one of those.

I looked at Quentin, who had collapsed onto the carpet. "What happened to you?" I asked him.

He snorted. "That dumb Poopsie ambushed me while I was having supper. She almost tore my wing off!" He flexed the injured appendage and squawked in pain. "So, do you have any meds to heal my wing?"

"I think so. Let me go check." I left Quentin sprawled out on the living room floor and went into the bathroom. I searched the medicine cabinet until I found the first aid kit I bought when I got my first flying animal, a winged horse named Jordan. "Okay,

Quentin," I ordered, "stand up and fold your injured wing to your side."

He hesitated, eyeing me with his eagle eyes. "I like you, Shelly, but you don't have a medical degree."

I grunted. Griffins don't usually talk, but this one was a rare exception. Once a one-hit-wonder elfin rock star named Quentin "QT" Tamself, Quentin was turned into a griffin by his enchantress fiancée who caught him rendezvousing with her best friend. Griffins are known for their promiscuity in the wild. When his ex was murdered, it was apparent that the elf would stay a griffin forever. Eddie and I are the only ones who know his true identity. Nobody else knows Quentin can talk. I sighed. This was one of those times when I wished he couldn't speak. "Oh, stop your whining, and do what I tell you."

"I left a message on Vinnie's phone informing him about his girlfriend's dog," Eddie said from the kitchen, "He probably won't get back to me as usual."

Quentin complied and let me bandage his wing. Afterward, he wandered out to the kitchen and sniffed the pizza on the table. "Are you guys finished eating?" he asked Eddie, who had put his cell phone back in his pocket.

"Do you want the rest of the pizza?" my husband asked him.

"Please?"

Eddie placed the pizza on the floor. "Put the pan in the sink when you're done, Quentin."

The griffin downed our meal in three bites and belched loudly. "Would it be okay if I sleep inside tonight? That Poopsie might kill me in my sleep."

Eddie hesitated. "I don't know, Quentin. Shelly might not be up to it."

I came into the kitchen and placed a hand on Eddie's forearm. "It'll be fine, honey," I assured him.

"Are you sure, babe?"

I nodded. "I just want to go to bed. Quentin, you can sleep on the living room floor."

The griffin padded out to the living room and settled down right in front of the stairs leading up to the loft. He turned around a few times before plopping down on the carpet and then tucked his head under his uninjured wing. Within moments he was snoring soundly.

Eddie and I crept past him and into our bedroom. I retrieved my nightgown from a dresser drawer and began to undress with my back to my husband. Out of habit, I looked at the dresser's mirror and remembered with a sigh that I now had no reflection.

"The scars you received from that gargoyle attack are completely gone," Eddie said softly as his fingers traced the invisible lines on my bareback.

I finished putting on the nightgown, saying nothing. I reached up and touched my completely healed throat. My mind flashed back to the vampire attack, and I staggered back at the recollection of the memory.

Eddie caught me. "You're all right?"

"I'm fine," I lied. "Just tired, that's all." I crawled into bed and pulled the covers up to my chin. I watched in silence as Eddie put on a pair of red drawstring pajama pants with no shirt. "Did you put a ward spell on the house?" I asked him.

"I did when you were up in the loft," he said as he slipped in next to me.

"Maybe it wore off when we let Quentin in. It could have worn off by now."

Eddie let out a semi-aggravated sigh. "Shell, I am the only one who can recant the spell, you know that."

"I know, I know. It's just that I'm afraid—." My voice trailed off as I decided not to worry my husband anymore.

"You're afraid that vampire might find you?" he asked.

I drew myself close to him. "Yeah," I whispered.

"He won't hurt you, babe. I won't let you down again."

I looked at him. "What do you mean by that?" When his only response was turning the bedside lamp off, I decided to get into his mind, but he immediately blocked my telepathy. What was he hiding from me? I sighed. We both needed a good night's sleep, and so I decided not to pursue the subject any further.

A woman in her twenties sits upon a silver throne. I can't see her face, but she looks familiar. "Diamondback, I don't care how you kill her! Just do it!" she shouts at the same vampire who attacked me in the alley.

He nods as he falls down on one knee in complete

respect. "It shall be done, your Majesty."

"Drain her if you must. I will take care of the Guardian."

I suddenly find myself back in the alley on that horrible night. The vampire knocks me down on the ground and begins tearing at my throat. "Eddie, help me! Eddie!" I scream desperately.

"Shelly, wake up!" Eddie said as he began shaking my shoulder.

My eyes were bathed in the harsh light of our bedside lamp the moment I opened them. "Where is he?"

"It's all right, babe," my husband reassured me as he pulled me closer. "Nobody's here but you and me. You just had a nightmare, that's all."

"A horrible nightmare," I said, trying to control my shaking body.

"Was it about the attack?"

I nodded as I told him about the dream. Well, only partially. I decided to leave out the scene with the mysterious queen. If I didn't understand my nightmare, my husband would be baffled as well. "I just can't get that night out my mind."

"Neither can I. . ." his voice trailed off as he turned on his back and stared up at the ceiling. He was doing it again, blocking his thoughts from me. What was he hiding from me?

I broke free of Eddie and got out of bed. I put on my blue satin robe and started to head out the door.

He propped himself up on one elbow. "Where are you going, Shell?" he asked.

"Just to the bathroom," I answered, reading the concern in his voice. "I'll be back in a few minutes, hon."

I shuffled into the living room, bathed in the glow of the midmorning sun, and nearly tripped over Quentin, who had planted himself right in front of the bathroom door. Instead of toppling on my head, I did a perfect somersault in the air and landed on my feet. *Okay, that was different*, I thought. I never had that much agility when I was human.

Maybe this whole vampire thing was going to turn out okay. Not many newly turned vampires were married to their mentors. Then again, not too many vampires are turned them against their will and left for dead.

I went into the bathroom and splashed cold water on my face and the back of my neck. A lump in my throat began to grow, and I leaned forward against the sink. Get ahold of yourself, Shelly, I told myself as I blinked back the tears. Whoever said vampires are soulless creatures are full of crap. We have feelings just like everyone else. I grabbed a hand towel and wiped my face and neck. I wasn't going to let Eddie know I felt like crying again.

I stepped out of the bathroom to hear banging on the front door. The now-working kitchen wall clock read ten-twenty. Morning for some, but in the middle of the night for us vampires. I grunted and peered through the massive curtained window of the front door. What was our landlord doing on our doorstep? I unlocked the door and opened it a crack, avoiding the sunlight. The sun's rays can easily blister a new vampire's skin within minutes. "What do you want, Vinnie?" I demanded.

The slimy satyr, reeking of stale Twinkies and too much beer, leered at me as he tried to suck in his potbelly gut. His thinning red hair was slicked back with sickly sweet pomade. The thirty-something slumlord had some of it on his horns. He wore jeans that bunched up in all the wrong places and a dirty white tank top. "Just a note to let you know I'm raising your rent. You and Eddie owe me $1,800 by next week."

"Why did you just triple our rent?"

"As your landlord, I don't have to offer you an explanation."

Translation: I'm doing something slightly illegal. "But you can't do that. We just renewed our lease last month."

"Lady, let me talk to the man of the house. He knows more about financial things."

How dare he insult me like that? Did he think I was some stupid bimbo? I was the one paying rent for over six years.

"Is everything all right, Shell?" Eddie asked as he came up behind me.

"No!" I nearly shouted. "Vinnie just tripled our rent, clearly violating our lease agreement."

The satyr shook his head at Eddie. "Women, all beauty, and no brains, huh?"

My husband glared at him. "Don't insult my wife. You can't raise our rent right after we renewed our lease."

"Sure, I can. I'm the landlord, and I can do whatever I want."

Eddie crossed his arms over his bare chest. "Not if we take legal actions."

He shrugged. "I'll just evict you. Just like those annoying pixies."

Righteous indignation surged through me like a flame to a pile of dry leaves. "The ones you killed with your toxic pesticides?" I snapped, baring my new fangs just to intimidate the scumbag. I was strongly considering snapping the slumlord's neck like a pathetic twig.

Eddie put a hand on my shoulder and pulled me back. "Shelly, he's not worth it," he said, reading my intentions. "Vinnie, get off our doorstep!"

"Well, it's my doorstep considering you're renting from me."

I heard my husband mutter, "Duracell!" A blue ball of energy appeared, hovering over one of his open palms. "Beat it, Vinnie!" he growled.

The satyr gave a nonchalant shrug as he walked away.

"Oh, by the way, new rule: no griffins!"

I slammed the door. "Who does that jerk think he is?" I asked.

"I think it's time to move."

"Can we terminate our lease?" I asked as the former wizard, now vampire, dropped the little ball of energy down the garbage disposal. "Is that ball going to damage the disposal?"

"Nah, this disposal tears up diamonds. A little ball of pure energy will just scratch it. I'll call around in the morning about getting some legal advice. For now, let's go back to bed." He put an arm around me and led me into the bedroom. As we lay in each other's arms, I tried to fall back asleep, but the bizarre, frightening dream and the encounter with our landlord kept me wide-awake.

Chapter Two:

Vampire Librarian Versus Robots

I forced myself to go to work a week later, even with Eddie's insistence that I give myself another day of rest. All this "rest" was making me restless, especially since I had been having the exact same nightmare repeatedly. Because I work the graveyard shift at the Zephyr Public Library, I missed the morning staff meeting. I checked my work email and groaned inwardly as I read the message from the director.

It wasn't great. The city of Zephyr was slicing budgets everywhere, and of course, the first place they hit was the library. There was an extremely high possibility that I was going to be one of many librarians laid off in the next few months. This month was definitely in the top ten "Worst Months of My Life" category. I forced back the tears all through my workday until dinner.

I called Eddie. "What's up, babe?" he asked.

I slowly stirred my soup. "I just found there is a strong chance I could be laid off," I said, choking back tears.

"Oh, Shelly! I'm so sorry!"

"I don't know what we're going to do if I get laid off."

"Shelly," Eddie said in a soft, reassuring voice, "we'll get through this."

I wiped away the tears with the heel of my hand. "I know, but this month has been crappy enough, and I can't handle anything else."

"Do you want me to come to take you home?"

I swallowed hard. "I'll be okay."

"You're sure?"

"Yeah."

"We don't have to go blood-tasting tonight. We'll do it some other night."

"No! I'm not drinking any of that nasty swamp rat blood!" I must have shouted because everyone in the break room looked up from their meals and stared at me.

"Shell?"

"I'm sorry, Eddie," I said, my voice barely above a whisper.

"It's okay. I'll see you at two."

"Yeah."

"I'll be there. I'm not going to be late ever again, I promise."

There it was again: the odd remark. Eddie was definitely hiding something from me. He had never apologized so profusely for being late. What had changed? Was it the attack? I would ask him about it when we got home. "I should let you go."

"Me too. I love you, Shelly."

"I love you, Eddie." There was silence. "Well, bye, honey."

"Bye, babe."

I hung up the phone and stared down at my now cold soup. I got up and dumped it into the trash. My appetite was gone, but I was able to finish off my soda. Most days, I prefer to be on the circulation desk interacting with customers, instead of putting away and rearranging books. Today, however, I was not happy to be working at the checkout counter. I didn't want to answer any unsolicited questions from patrons asking how I became a vampire or about the massive budget cuts.

"Oh, my dear, you have become one of us!" said Norma Alucard, a vampire in her six hundreds (or sixties for you humans) who was an avid cozy mystery reader. She put her usual pile of twenty books on the counter.

"Yes," I replied as I plastered a fake smile on my face.

"What kind of blood did you choose?"

I hesitated as I began scanning each individual library barcode right before I slipped the slip of cardstock with the due date into the pocket. "Well, I haven't picked a blood type yet. My husband and I are going to a few places for blood-tasting."

"Oh, which stores?"

I shrugged. "Don't know yet. Do you have any recommendations?"

She nodded. "Well, the only store that Harold and I get our blood from is Trader Drac's. Let me give you the address." She pulled a piece of paper and a pen from her gigantic embroidered purse and jotted down the address, which she handed to me. "Now, when you go there, tell Sol I sent you. He has the best blood prices in town."

I glanced past her the moment I heard the high pitched alarm go off. An elfin teenager in a gray hoodie hunched over from the weight of his backpack. He carried his skateboard in one arm as he shuffled through the security gates. "Excuse me," I said to Mrs. Alucard. "Sir! Sir!" I called loudly to the teenager. "Excuse me! Come back here, please."

Suddenly he bolted out the door, shoving past a mother holding her little girl. The righteous indignation at library book thieves came over me. I vaulted over the four-and-half-foot tall desk and began to run after the little punk. "Stop!" I shouted at him.

He ran down the marble steps and onto the street. He let his skateboard fall to the ground, jumped on, and pushed off with his left foot. He turned and shot an uncomplimentary gesture towards me.

"Rat-faced little punk!" I snarled. Without thinking, I leaped down the entire marble staircase, a total of twenty-five steps, and landed gracefully on the sidewalk. Whoa! Sweet vampire power! I began to run after the library thief who had just turned down a side street. "Stop! Thief!" I shouted. And just like in the movies, nobody stopped him. He crossed another road and skateboarded under the belly of a giant, ten-foot-high ant. The driver, a young vampire in her early teens, screamed an obscenity at my quarry as she tried to regain control of her now bucking and extremely startled insect.

"Watch it, lady!" he shouted nastily at her.

The vampire was clearly an inexperienced insect rider as she gave a sharp tug to the right. The ant lost its footing and began to tumble in front of me. Without breaking stride, I hurdled over the girl and her tumbling bug like a track star. The moment I landed on the ground almost cat-like, I glanced back in surprise. "I did not just jump over a ten-foot bug!" I said to myself as I resumed the pursuit with a wide grin.

I yanked back on the cloth loop on the top of his backpack, pulling the kid off his skateboard. "Gotcha!" I said triumphantly.

"What the heck, lady?" he snapped as I spun him around to face me. "Why you be all up in my grill?" Oh my word, I had encountered the worst gangsta wannabe ever. He was wearing a blue backward baseball cap over a red and black bandanna. His baggy jeans hung halfway down his backside, his tighty whities exposed to the world. Around his neck, he wore an obnoxiously huge fake gold chain with an equally obnoxious gold pendant marked "R." "I've got rights, fool!" he said as he made a bunch of purely made-up hand gestures.

"Why didn't you stop when I asked you?"

He crossed his arms defiantly. "I wasn't doing anything! Know what I'm sayin', fool?"

I held up my hand. "Drop the gangsta talk, homeboy," I told him. "It's mildly irritating."

He sighed. "Yes, ma'am."

"Open up your backpack. Please, for the love of Pete, pull up your pants!"

He grunted as he slid it off his shoulder and unzipped one of the five compartments. "It's just my own books," he said with a new surly teenager attitude. "I bought them with my own money."

I fished the eight books out and looked them over. Stamped on the top edge of the book in big, black letters were the words: Zephyr Public Library. "These are library books. What's your name, kid?"

"Lawrence, but my friends call me 'Rambo' 'cause I strike fear into everyone I meet. You can't prove that those books are from the library!"

This kid was dumb as a post. I pointed to the stamp at the top. "Yes, I can. It's right there."

"Well, I'm holding them for a friend."

I opened one of the books and showed him the empty pocket on the back cover. "Then why is there no due date slip in here?"

"He forgot them?"

"Right, how about we take these books back to the library and tell your 'friend' that you have his books at the circulation desk."

He sighed with the realization that he had been caught red-handed. "Oh, come on, lady. They're just library books. They're free!"

"No!" I snapped, fed up with this little punk's attitude towards libraries. "They are not free! The library has to order them and process them so that people who actually appreciate them have the opportunity to read them without stealing!"

He gave an exaggerated yawn. "Yeah, yeah, I know how the library works. My dad is on the board."

I gave a fanged grin. "Good, then we can call and tell him all about you stealing library books." The kid tried to make a break for it, but I caught him by the ear. "Rambo, I just chased you for three blocks and jumped over a giant ant, all without breaking a sweat. I wouldn't try to run if I were you." I began to drag him back to the library by the ear. All the while, he was kicking and screaming like a five-year-old.

Two blurs of black and red started to race towards us and then suddenly screeched to a halt. I zoned into the newcomers using my newfound vampire senses. No heat signatures whatsoever. Even zombies give off pale blue heat signatures. The shapes were definitely humanoid, but something was definitely wrong. I barely had time to think about it when two plasma blasts erupted out of nowhere. "Get down!" I yelled to the kid as I threw both of us down to the sidewalk. Rambo, the fearless, began shrieking like a little girl. Shaking my head in disgust, I activated my bracelet just as the blasts bounced off the impenetrable metal shield.

"Exterminate! Exterminate the usurper!" the creatures chanted in a robotic voice. They came running at us. They launched themselves effortlessly over parked animals and insects. One of them rammed a metal fist in the concrete, creating a powerful earthquake effect. Windows shattered, and buildings shook.

My vision narrowed into a binocular-like view for a few minutes until I got a clear picture of our visitors. The things were twenty-foot versions of Robocop (except for being entirely mechanical.) They had guns for hands, which were now shooting more plasma rays at us. Crap. No wonder I couldn't get a heat signature. They weren't even human. Robots were attacking us.

I reached into my pants pocket and pulled out Knowledge in her book form. Rambo let out another shriek. "A book! You're a freakin' vampire, and your only weapon is a book!" he shrieked hysterically.

"Get to somewhere safe!" I ordered him before saying the magical incantation. Green sparks appeared around the book as it morphed into a deadly blade. I unsheathed the sword and hung the sheath across my back. One of the robots held up its hands, and two lasers shot out from its palms. I rolled out of the way just in time as the backpack next to me disintegrated into ashes. "Lawrence!" I shouted to the terrified gangsta who was crouching behind a mailbox. "Get someplace safe!"

"What about my backpack?"

"Not important!" I snapped. "Now, go or stay here and fight!"

"I'll go!" He took off into a run and disappeared around a corner. Apparently, chivalry had died with this teenager a long time ago. I calculated my odds of surviving, which were incredibly slim. "Okay, Knowledge, you can deflect magic. Let's see if you can cut through metal." The robots were about a couple yards away. Good, I had a running start. If I could jump over giant ants with ease, then kicking robot butt would be a piece of cake.

Placing my shield in front of my body, I broke into a run towards the robots. More throwing stars came at me with deadly accuracy, and I bent backward, Matrix-style, as they spun inches over my shielded body. Then I jumped in mid-air at the first robot who fired another round of lasers at me. I somersaulted out of harm's way before taking off its head in one fluid arch with Knowledge. He fell to the ground in a dispatched heap of wires and metal. This sword was a lot sharper than I thought, or I was stronger than I realized.

I landed on the ground in a cat-like crouch in front of Robot Number Two and cut off both legs with another über-strong sweep of my sword. I rolled out of the way to avoid being crushed by the falling robot. The red bulbs for the robots' eyes flickered and then went out. I took a fighting stance and listened with my new vamp super-hearing for any more signs of robots, but nothing. I had gotten rid of the danger for now. I couldn't wait to tell my husband about my cool, new abilities.

Eddie was waiting for me in the car when I got off work at the end of my shift. His royal blue dress shirt was rolled up just past the elbows. He wore black jeans and black leather boots. "So, are you feeling any better?" he asked as we kissed.

I was still psyched from my battle. "You'll never believe what happened to me!"

"What? Are you alright?"

"I'm fine, but wow!" Then I excitedly told him about the encounter with the robots. "Isn't this cool? I've never felt so good in my life."

"No!" my husband snapped with a sudden angry edge to his voice. "It isn't cool. Good God, Shelly! What were you thinking? You could have been killed!"

"I was just trying to recover some stolen library books, Eddie," I said softly.

"Library books aren't worth risking your life!" he answered.

"I can take care of myself!" I snapped back.

"And what if the next time you go cavorting into danger, you can't take care of yourself?"

"I don't go 'cavorting' into danger. Those robots attacked me, not the other way around! Plus, you've done dangerous stuff in your life, and I've never complained."

"It's different for me!"

"Oh, don't pull that 'I used to be a spy, and therefore I can be in dangerous situations' crap with me, Eddie! Or have you forgotten the reason you gave me Knowledge was so I could protect myself when you aren't around."

"The sword wasn't an invitation for you to go fight things all by yourself without me watching your back."

"I'm a vampire, and—."

"For Pete's sake, Shelly! We vamps aren't invincible!"

"Thanks a lot, Eddie," I said bitterly as I crossed my arms over my chest.

"For what?" he asked through gritted teeth.

"I was looking forward to a pleasant evening of blood-tasting with you, and you have completely ruined it."

"I wasn't the one who—."

"Just shut up and take me home!"

When we got home, we still hadn't spoken to each other. Eddie slammed the front door behind us and went to our bedroom. A few minutes later, he came out wearing his leather motorcycle gloves and a jean jacket. He tucked his helmet tucked under his arm. "Where are you going?" I harshly demanded.

"For a ride!" he snapped back.

"When are you going to be back?"

"I don't know! If you decide to get into danger, at least give me a heads up!" With that surly comment, he headed out, slamming the door behind him a second time. I heard his motorcycle rev up before he peeled rubber out of our little driveway.

I rummaged angrily through our kitchen for food. I found leftover meatless lasagna Eddie had made the night before. I heated up a piece for myself and ate only a few bites with a couple of swallows of that nasty swamp rat blood before putting the bottle back in the fridge. The fight with my husband had left me with no appetite.

I started to clean up the kitchen when my cell phone rang. For a moment, I thought it was Eddie calling to apologize, but then I realized it wasn't his unique ringtone. "Hello?" I said glumly.

"Shelly, how are you?" said my sister-in-law, Lisa Van Helsing.

"Fine," I lied.

"So, have you and Eddie bought a gift for my dad's wedding?"

I struggled to fight back the tears. "No!" I said, choking back a sob.

"Are you okay, Shelly?"

I swallowed hard. "Eddie and I had a fight." I hesitantly told her about the fight. "I don't know why he's angry with me. He's never been like this before," I told her once I was finished.

"Well, maybe he's right," Lisa suggested.

"What do you mean?"

"You should try to be more feminine. Guys really feel inadequate when their girls are off fighting robots and putting themselves in danger. Talk to him and make him feel special."

I gritted my teeth. *Thanks for being so condescending, Lisa*, I thought angrily to myself. I managed to hide my anger. "He is special, but ever since the attack, he has been acting strange."

"Dirk, stop it!" she said with a giggle. "Shelly, I have to go! Dirk's getting antsy."

"All right, thanks for talking, Lisa. Bye." I hung up the phone and headed to the kitchen. I opened a new container of chocolate chip cookie dough ice cream. At least I never have to worry about gaining weight.

"Shelly, if I say I'm sorry, would you be willing to share your ice cream?"

I looked up from my second tub of ice cream at my husband, who sat across from me with a spoon in his hand. He set his motorcycle helmet on the edge of the table. I didn't even hear him come in.

"Sure," I replied as I pushed the half-eaten container over to him.

He took a bite of the mint chocolate chip ice cream. "I'm so sorry about earlier tonight," he said quietly. "I shouldn't have shouted at you."

"I'm sorry, too," I replied. "I didn't mean any of those things."

"Neither did I. It's just that. . ." His voice trailed off as he indulged himself in another scoop.

I couldn't stand it any longer. I hated seeing my husband like this. Something was bothering him, and I had to find out. "Eddie, what's really going on? Please, tell me, honey."

He sighed. "I'm so sorry I was late."

"For what?" I asked, perplexed. I could see the tears running down his cheeks. "What's wrong?"

He wiped away the tears. "The night you were attacked, I was late, Shell. I should've been there. I could've stopped him. I'm so sorry for not being there for you."

"Oh, Eddie!" My heart started to break for my husband. I held his hand. "I didn't know."

"There was an incident at the diner. I tried to get away, but I just couldn't. My heart nearly broke in two when the hospital called me at the diner. Did you know you were dead for six minutes? I thought I had lost you. It was the worst six minutes of my life. Even with the blood transfusions, I didn't know if you were going to make it."

We were silent for two or three long moments as I took in what my husband had told me. "Eddie, I have something to tell you," my voice quavered with emotion. "That night, I left my sword and shield on the kitchen table. I didn't think I needed them. I didn't even sense him until it was too late. I tried to fight him off, Eddie, I really did."

"I know."

"That's why I had to fight those robots. I wasn't going to be a victim again."

"The next time you encounter danger, I want to be there, fighting alongside you."

"I want you to be there."

Eddie pushed the ice cream back to me with a warm smile. "So, what do you want for supper other than ice cream?"

"I think this is a great supper," I said, returning the smile.

Chapter Three:
I Find a Lost Pixie

"Doctor Goodelf, why did they fail?" she yells at the old man in the white lab coat. It's the same woman I have been dreaming about.

"If you hadn't cut back on the robots' outer shells, they most definitely would have killed her, Queen Rachel."

"Don't talk back to me, you insolent worm!" she screams. "Or do you want to end up like your sister?" With a flick of her wrist, an image appears of a yellow-eyed vampire tearing open the throat of an elfin woman. "Diamondback has been thirsty lately. Doctor, make sure the next set of robots can't be taken apart by a little knife."

I woke up with a gasp. I sat up in bed and wrapped my

arms around myself to stop the trembling.

"Shelly, are you okay?" Eddie asked. My sudden movement in bed had awoken him. He flicked on the nightstand lamp on his side of the bed. "Did you have another nightmare?"

"Maybe," I said, shaking my head, "I don't know."

"Do you want to talk about it?"

I lay back in Eddie's arms. "Yeah, I guess so." This time, I told him everything that happened in the dream. When I mentioned the name "Diamondback," his face turned ashen.

"What's wrong, hon?" I asked.

"Are you sure the woman referred to him as 'Diamondback?'"

"Yes, I'm positive. Who is he?"

Eddie swallowed hard as he tried to formulate the next sentence in his mind before speaking. "Diamondback is a trained assassin." My mouth fell open in shock, but I said nothing and let my husband continue. "The Agency pegged him to be over 800-years-old."

"Was he bitten or born a vampire?" I asked.

He nodded. "We think he was bitten. We never knew his

real name. He got that name because of the way he attacked his victims, silent and swift like a snake.”

“You knew him?”

“Not directly. I led an all-vampire team to take down Diamondback after he massacred a government official and his entire family. The Agency figured eight vampires could kill a single vampire. My team and I barely survived the mission. I was one of three survivors. Ever since then, Diamondback has been off the grid.” He paused. Eddie rarely talks about his days as a spy for an international intelligence agency. His reasoning is because it could compromise various missions, but I suspect he participated in missions he’d preferred not to share with me. He formed his next sentence carefully. “I think Diamondback was after me, and he attacked you to get my attention.”

I shook my head. “I don’t think so.”

“What do you mean?”

“Right before he bit me, he said, ‘This is for the queen.’ Plus, the woman in my dream referred to him.”

“Well, do you know anyone named Rachel?”

“No.” I squeezed my eyes shut in frustration. “I’m tired,

hon. Let's go back to sleep."

"Sounds like a good idea." Eddie kissed me before turning out the light. "I love you, Shelly," he whispered as he caressed my cheek.

I ran my fingers through his curly, black hair. "I love you, too, Eddie."

We lay quietly in the darkness for a while until I broke the silence. "Eddie?"

"Yeah?"

"Did you ever have weird dreams when you became a vampire?"

"No, but your dreams could be a sign of post-traumatic stress disorder."

I snuggled close to him. "Maybe. I just can't get the dreams out of my mind."

"Well," he said suggestively, "I do know a way to get them temporarily off your mind."

I gave a little laugh. "Hmm. Enticing offer, dear. I accept."

While at work the following day, I decided to use my

librarian skills to look up anything related to my dreams. First, I went to the Internet (Hey, don't give me that look! We librarians travel the information superhighway all the time as a legitimate research tool.) I typed "Doctor Goodelf" into the search engine, Findit.com, and after sifting through various links about doctors, elves, and even Dr. Feelgood, I came across an interesting article.

According to the Wixom Daily News, Dr. Luther Goodelf was a renowned engineer in Wixom, a metropolis twice the size of Zephyr, in their robotic weapons department when he lost the opportunity to lead a team of scientists to build a robotic arm with nuclear capabilities. These devices would be attached to the soldiers during combat. The government decided to shut down his department after deeming his project "unsafe to all involved." Dr. Goodelf didn't take rejection lightly and went postal with his nuclear toy, blowing up the entire base and killing himself along with fifty other people. Goodelf was dead, or so it seemed. The authorities were still looking for his body over the past ten years. The very last sentence of the article was what really caught my attention: "This is the eighteenth disappearance of a high profile criminal in the past six months."

I clicked on the various links, praying that they wouldn't lead me down paths of computer viruses and spyware. What they did connect me to was more articles about mob bosses, serial killers, dirty politicians, and various other kinds of nefarious criminal types, all of whom had gone off the grid in the past ten years. It was odd, but my gut told me there was a connection somewhere in this muddled mess.

The next subject I searched for was the person known in my dream as Queen Rachel. I got zilch. "I don't get it," I said quietly. "How can there be no record of any kind of queen?" I couldn't shake the feeling that I somehow knew her, but for the life of me, I couldn't even begin to guess how or why I knew this so-called Queen Rachel.

The closest I had ever come to royalty was Eddie's aunt and uncle, the Count and Countess Von Stoker, and they're about as royal as the King of Pop. The only reason they held those titles is that the Countess, or "Aunt Phoebe," as she likes me to call her, comes from a long line of aristocratic vampires. I highly doubt she knows any queens, but then again, she is over

500-years-old.

While on my break, I grabbed my cell phone and scrolled through my contacts until I reached the home number for Aunt Phoebe and Uncle Konrad. I hit the send button and tapped my fingers on the table in the staff lounge as I waited for someone to pick up on the other end. "Von Stoker residence," said a deep, rumbling voice.

It took me a minute to recognize the voice of their new butler. What was his name? Perkins, that was it. "Hi, Perkins. Is Phoebe there?"

"Whom may I say is calling?"

"Her niece, Shelly Van Helsing."

"One moment, please," he said as he put me on hold. I didn't have to wait long. "Hello?" said a matronly voice.

"Aunt Phoebe?"

"Shelly, how are you and Eddie?"

"Good," I said. "Um, I have a question."

"Go ahead, dear."

I formulated the question in my mind before speaking it

aloud. "Do you know anyone called Queen Rachel?"

"No!" she seemed surprised at my question. "Why? Are you and Eddie in some kind of trouble?"

"Oh, no! Not at all! Just a name I heard in passing." It was a half-truth, but I really felt uncomfortable telling her exactly where I heard the name. Hey, Aunt Phoebe, I had a crazy dream where I listened to my attacker talk with a chick who thought she was some kind of queen. "How are you and Uncle Konrad?"

"Wonderful! We must have you and Eddie over for dinner sometime."

"Yeah, that'd be great. I'll talk to Eddie and get back to you."

"Shelly, I have to let you go. Konrad and I are playing bridge with some friends, and I should get back to them. Good-bye, dear."

"Good-bye, Aunt Phoebe," I said as I hung up.

I went back to eating my chocolate bar when the staff phone began to ring. I looked around and concluded I was the only one who was even looking at the phone. I went over and picked it up. "Staffroom," I said into the receiver.

"Shelly?" It was one of the library pages, Jenna. "There is a pixie woman here to see you."

"I'll be right up," I said, hanging up the phone. The only pixie woman I knew was Addison Cloude, the matriarch of the pixie family who once inhabited the flowerbeds next to our house. Maybe they were all still alive and safe somewhere. I jogged up the back stairs to the front desk where a pixie woman no more than five inches tall was zipping nervously back and forth between the circulation desk and the display of gardening books.

She wore a tiny green peasant shirt and a gray broomstick skirt that twirled as she flew. Her long, blond hair wasn't up in its usual tie-dyed bandana. Instead, it cascaded over her shoulders and down her back. Silver pixie dust continuously plummeted to the marble floor from her transparent dragonfly wings. She wasn't even controlling her pixie dust. Something was terribly wrong.

"Addison?" I asked as I came around the counter.

"Shelly, have you seen Raine?" she immediately asked without even so much as a hello.

"No, in fact, I haven't seen any of you guys since your flowerbed was destroyed." I gave a sigh of relief. "At least, you guys are okay. Eddie and I are really worried about you."

"Raine's been missing for over a week!"

I gasped. "What?"

"She went to tell you about the trouble we were having with Poopsie, and then she was supposed to stay with her grandparents that weekend," Tears began to fill the hazel eyes of the single mother of twenty kids. "But my mother told me she never showed up." At this point, her shoulders sagged, and she began to sob little pixie sobs. "And the police haven't been very helpful. They think that she just ran away."

I was about to say something when an image flashed in my mind. In my mind's eye, I saw my attacker shield his eyes from a flash of pure sunlight coming from a teenage pixie with bright purple hair and matching eyes. She immediately passed out and dropped into the open dumpster below her. The image faded from my mind as quickly as it came. I opened my closed eyes and looked at Addison. "I know where Raine is!" I said.

"Are you sure my daughter's in there?" Addison asked, eying the black dumpster. We were standing at the entrance of an all-too-familiar alley. "What if she has been taken to the dump when they came to collect the garbage?"

"Everyone forgets about this alley," I told her. Except for assassins, but I kept that thought to myself. I took a baby step into the bleak alley. *Get a grip on yourself, Shelly*, I told myself. *He's not here. This isn't even about you. It's a rescue mission.* I steeled myself before entering. "Addison, stay here." I closed my eyes. When I opened my eyes, I noticed something was off. A dark ring surrounded the edges of my vision. I rubbed my eyes vigorously for a few moments until the binocular-like feeling vanished. Weird.

I shook my head and focused on my new vampire super hearing for anything that shouldn't belong in a deserted alley. My new auditory skills zeroed in on a heartbeat coming from somewhere in the dumpster. I flung open the top and scanned the array of trash. That's when I spotted the green heat signature of a teenage pixie. "Raine!"

The teenager was pinned against the side of the smelly,

metal container, encased in a sleeping bag of pink gum. "Help!" she moaned groggily.

"Raine, it's Shelly! Are you okay?"

"What does it look like?" she snapped back at me.

I smiled. The kid was going to be okay. "Sorry." I turned back to the anxious Addison. "I found her!"

Addison zipped over to the dumpster. "Oh, Raine!" Once she got a look at her daughter, she screamed. "How are we going to get her out of there? She could die!"

"Geesh, Mom! It's not like I've been gone forever," the teenager rolled her eyes.

"Don't talk back to me, young lady! I have been looking for you all week."

"Really, an entire week?" Raine asked in disbelief.

"You must have gone into your hibernation state," I said as I looked around for something sharp enough to pry the pixie off the wall. When pixies use a large amount of their magic all at once, their bodies automatically go into a hibernation-like state to recover and heal. This deep sleep can last up to three weeks.

I tore open a garbage bag and pawed through its contents

until I found a food encrusted, melted plastic spatula, and a half-empty bottle of water. I shook the bottle until it became cold. "This should work," I said as I unscrewed the cap. "Close your eyes, Raine." I began to pour the water on top of her, turning the gum hard. Within a few seconds, I chipped Raine off the side of the dumpster, catching her with my free hand.

She tried to stand but fell clumsily into my palm. Probably dizzy from hunger. Addison came over and hugged her daughter. "Are you okay?" she asked.

"Yeah, just really hungry," Raine replied as she looked up at me. "Hey, Shelly, your eyes look funny. Like a kitty cat."

The binocular feeling came back, but I shut my eyes again until it went away. I was more worried about Raine's condition. Maybe she had a concussion. Something could have hit her head when she was in her hibernation state. "My eyes are fine. Addison, you should really take her to the hospital."

"Don't worry about Raine," Addison assured me as she helped her daughter back on her feet. "Temporary confusion is common when coming out of a pixie hibernation state. But I will take her to the hospital." She gave a series of short, two-finger whistles before a sparrow flew by. The two pixies climbed on the bird's back. The mother turned to me. "We're staying at the fifth flowerbed on the left at Zephyr Memorial Park."

I frowned. Pixies living in the city parks' flowerbed meant only thing: homelessness. I desperately wanted to help the Cloudes, but inviting them back to my house would only endanger their lives. "Eddie and I will come by later on to see you guys," I assured her and watched them fly away.

Chapter Four:
Blood-tasting Can Be Hazardous to Your Health

Nothing else happened during my shift. I realized that Eddie and I still hadn't bought a wedding gift for our friends. Even though I have known Bruce Miller most of my life, I'm much closer to his daughter, Lisa (who is now my sister-in-law), and his son, Roger. It was both Bruce and his wife-to-be, Libby Elfstar's second wedding, and my husband and I still had no idea what to get them. Every gift on their registry was too expensive for us or had already been bought. Serves us right for not buying the present earlier. After bouncing ideas off my fellow coworkers, I finally decided on a gift card to a fancy housewares department store named Bed and Bath Emporium.

Eddie was waiting for me when I got out of work. I opened the back door of his waiting carrot-shaped car, tossed my blue and purple striped tote bag onto the back seat, and shut the door before getting into the passenger seat. I placed my purse at my feet and gave my husband a "hello kiss." "How was your day?" I asked him.

"Odd," he said as he shifted the car into reverse and backed out of the parking lot. "We had a vampire come in, and you wouldn't believe what he was wearing."

"Nothing?" I guessed.

"Fortunately, he was fully clothed. He was decked out in some kind of 1940's air force uniform. He even had an eye patch over his right eye."

"Maybe he was going to a costume party."

Eddie shook his head. "I don't think so. The outfit looked pretty worn. I will say everyone noticed him, even me. The red beret he was wearing had the same symbol that's on your shield."

"The blue lion surrounded by the three fleurs-de-lis?"

"Yeah, I asked him about it, and he said he used to be an

officer for some royal family.”

“Okay, then!”

“Yeah, he was about to tell me more when a satyr came up to him and asked him to stop talking to me.”

“Weird.”

“It gets weirder.” Eddie took a right on Riverview Street before continuing. “The satyr was wearing a three-piece suit and a bowler hat. He was very distinguished-looking. ”

I gave my husband a surprised look. “A three-piece suit?” My dad’s restaurant was geared towards families, not some high-end dining establishment with minuscule portions. “Nobody ever wears a suit to the diner.”

“I know. I was surprised. Anyway, Amelia came out of the back office, took one look at both the vampire and satyr, and raced back inside.”

“Out of fear?”

He shook his head. “No, I think she recognized them.”

“That doesn’t surprise me, hon. Amelia’s been here as long as my family has.”

He shook his head again. “I don’t know, babe. Timothy

came out of the office with Amelia and told both of them to leave immediately."

"No way would Dad ever do that, especially to paying customers!"

"I know! I was shocked!" He pulled into the parking lot of the first blood store we were hitting. "Did you print off the right directions to Mainly Veinly last night?"

"This is what the internet gave me," I said hesitantly as I glanced around the postage-stamp-sized parking lot. The one street light attempted to give off a sense of safety but decided to burn itself out from despair. Roving gangs of delinquent teenagers had decided to decorate every building with random expressions of typical teenage angst. Eddie and I exchanged skeptical looks. "Maybe the inside is a lot nicer," I suggested hopefully.

"Doubtful," he replied as we got out of the car. He hit the automatic lock and then said a protection spell, "Contengo!"

"Not taking any chances, are we?" I asked.

He smiled as he took my hand in his. "I don't want to see my car stripped down to the axles."

The second we entered the store, I felt like I should've been wearing body armor. The first clue was the front door with wrought iron bars running down its length. The top panel, or what was left of it, had so many cracks that the slightest movement might shatter the remaining glass. A piece of plywood had been haphazardly placed where the bottom glass panel should have been.

The interior was about the size of a gas station restroom, and not much cleaner. Our feet crunched along the not naturally gray floor. It took me a few seconds to realize that we were walking on the tiny exoskeletons of cockroaches. Forget the body armor, I should have been wearing a hazmat suit.

Bottles of blood lined three mounted bookcases. My eyes scanned the labels with amazement. "Wow, I didn't realize how many different kinds of animal blood are out there!" I said. "Dragon blood, sheep blood, pig, elephant, griffin, shark—Hey!" My eyes narrowed in suspicion as I read some more labels. "Pookendilly blood?" I looked at Eddie. "What is a pookendilly?"

"Maybe it's a kind of lizard?" he suggested with strong uncertainty.

"You don't know, do you?"

He shook his head. He looked at some of the other bottles. "What about a sibmoof? And a foapsat? I've never even heard of a moonjax."

I gave a laugh. "That last one sounds like a breakfast cereal. What about a thuzzle?" I pulled out my cell phone and surfed the net for the various kinds of blood. I showed my lack of answers to Eddie. "These aren't even real words!"

He glanced over his shoulder through the front door's window to make sure the car had not been stripped down to a skeletal carriage. "That brings two questions to mind. First, why is the owner making up fake animals? And second, what type of blood is in the bottles?"

"I know. It's really odd." Out of the corner of my eye, I saw something move behind the bottles "I think the owner must have a cat or something," I told Eddie.

He nodded as one of the bottles fell, splattering foul-smelling blood all over the floor. "I hope he knows that his cat is playing behind his merchandise."

I let out a small shriek as a pointed, whiskery nose poked

through the space made by the fallen bottle. "That's no cat!"

"Shelly, don't freak out," Eddie said as a slime-green rat the size of a housecat emerged from its hiding place, sending more bottles to their fate. Foul-smelling blood pooled on the floor.

I started backing towards the door. I hate, hate, hate rodents of all sizes. "Let's get out of here!"

"It might be his pet rat!"

The door behind the grimy wooden counter swung open, and a beefy, sweaty vampire in a bloodstained, ratty old t-shirt and torn jeans (not the ones you buy pre-torn) emerged. "Oh, flux!" he said as he took one look at the rat now leaping onto the countertop. "I thought I got rid of these!" He grabbed the rat by the tail with one hand as he reached under the counter with the other one and pulled up a large meat cleaver. The rodent squealed with impending doom. With one swift, practiced swipe, he sliced the rat's throat as Eddie and I looked on in horror. Arterial spray scattered across his dirty shirt, and thankfully missed us.

He set the cleaver down and opened a bottle with a blank label from a shelf behind the counter. Turning the dead rat upside down, he let the remaining stinky blood drain into the container. A few seconds later, he screwed the cap back on and tossed the dead rat behind him, where it landed on the floor with a thump. He scribbled something on the bottle and set it neatly on the shelf.

I read the label and cringed: Dragon Blood. Our questions were answered.

"What can I get for you folks?" he asked, finally noticing his two shell-shocked customers. "Are you looking for some blood? 'Cause I got the best blood prices in town!" he said as he wiped his bloodied hands on his shirt and jeans. "Name's Bucky!" He reached out to shake my husband's hand.

Eddie quickly held up his hands. "You know what, babe?" he said to me. "We are lost!"

It took me a few seconds to figure out what Eddie was doing. "You're right, dear!" I replied as my brain decided to catch up with me. "We should have turned left at Albuquerque."

Eddie shot me an utterly puzzled look.

"At Albuquerque Street," I said, grasping at straws.

Bucky's skeptical look clearly indicated he knew of no

such street.

Eddie grabbed my elbow and steered me towards the door. "If we leave now, we'll make our reservation."

"Thanks for everything!" I called Bucky over my shoulder as we almost ran out the door. "Have a nice day!"

Once we were outside, Eddie looked at me. "'Thanks for everything?' What was that all about?"

"Sorry," I apologized as we walked back to the car. "I automatically say that whenever I leave a store." I shuddered at our recent experience.

"That was traumatizing," Eddie said

I nodded in agreement. "I hate rats, but I kind of felt sorry for the little rodent."

"I'm shocked the guy's even in business."

I saw something move in the shadows down the street. My eyesight did another weird binocular thing, and for a moment, I could clearly see a raccoon digging through a pail of garbage. I rubbed my eyes with the heels of my palms until the binocular feeling disappeared.

"Are you all right, Shelly?" Eddie asked as soon as he

undid the ward spell and unlocked the car.

"I think so," I replied unconvincingly as I got into the passenger seat.

"Are you sure?"

"I don't know, maybe. I keep getting this feeling like I'm looking through a pair of binoculars."

"How long has it been going on?" Eddie asked as he turned over the engine but didn't take the car out of park.

"Off and on all day."

"You could be suffering from blood dehydration."

"That's possible," I said. *According to Vampirism for Dummies*, new vampires need to drink about 6-8 glasses of blood a day for the first few weeks, and 1-2 glasses a day afterward. I only had two glasses at breakfast this morning. However, I wasn't feeling any other signs of dehydration: extreme thirst, dizziness, massive headaches, dry mouth, etc. "Well, what blood store should we hit next?" I asked.

Eddie gave me a concerned look. "You up to it?"

"I'm fine."

"Well, we could just buy a couple bottles from Bucky back

there and call it a night."

"Eww! Why would I drink blood from a store that probably has never passed any kind of inspections? I counted at least twenty health code violations."

"Thirty," Eddie added.

I dug into my purse and pulled out a pen and two sheets of paper containing a list of blood stores. I triple-crossed off Mainly Veinly off the list and looked down at the name below it. "Veindrain. That sounds promising."

"Let's go," Eddie replied as he shifted the car into drive, "What's the address?"

"Sixteen Grove Street. Sounds quaint."

As it turned out, Sixteen Grove Street was not in the least bit quaint. The medium-sized parking lot and the side streets were so packed that we ended up parking two blocks away. I took that to be a good sign. No parking spots meant great business, right? When we were only a few yards from the entrance, I saw a vampire with the figure of a bodybuilder checking IDs at the door.

Eddie looked at me. "Are we at a club?"

I glanced down at the paper in my hand. "Nope, it says here Veindrain is an exclusive blood store catering to the young, hip vampire crowd." I felt the ground shake beneath my feet. Was Zephyr experiencing an earthquake?

"Dude!" a vampire in his teens with multiple facial piercings shouted to his friend, "I love this song!"

Song? Then I heard faint musical notes of a sort drift through the air. The music continued to get louder and louder as we trudged towards the entrance. Finally, Mr. Olympia wanna-be demanded our IDs.

Eddie dug out his wallet and showed his license. "What's up with the ID checking?" he asked.

Mr. Olympia snorted. "Newbies, huh?"

"My wife is new," Eddie said as I showed Rippling Muscles my license.

"Veindrain offers blood and alcohol drinks." He explained as he barely glanced at our IDs and waved us in.

We were nearly blinded by the million strobe lights that caught us like a deer in headlights. "Holy crap!" I said to Eddie. "I think my tunnel vision just cleared up with my sudden blindness!"

I grabbed his arm so I wouldn't get lost in the throng of vampires.

"What?" he attempted to shout over the roar of people and the incredibly loud music.

Once the spots cleared from my eyesight, I got a look around. The place was about the size of a university lecture hall, but instead of a lectern on the stage, there was an eardrum-blowing band calling themselves the Invisible Klown Klones. Each of the five members was dressed exactly alike. Their faces were painted entirely white, which made the eighteen-and-nineteen-year-old vampires even paler. Four, thin, black lines were drawn horizontally across their lips. They had gone for the ever-stylish bright orange spiked Mohawk look, and it looked like a piercing bomb had exploded in their faces.

"Gross," I said the moment I saw the shirtless band drenched in fake blood.

What are they singing? Eddie telepathically asked me. He had given up trying to have a decent conversation with the incredibly loud music as background noise. They sound like they're growling. I feel sorry for their vocal cords.

I shook my head as I winced in pain, barely catching my husband's subliminal question. The deafening noise was wreaking havoc on my telepathy. Usually, I can control it by concentrating on a few minds at a time. Eddie had taught me that trick, but now my telepathy was spiraling into madness. "Get out of my head!" I screamed as thousands of uncensored thoughts from every single vampire in the room flooded into my mind. I fell to my knees in agony. Surprisingly, only Eddie noticed my predicament.

Shelly, what's wrong?

I. Can't. Concentrate. Telepathy. Going. Haywire. Every word I sent out to my husband was painfully hard. Tears squeezed out of my eyes.

Eddie knew immediately what to do. Pulling me to my feet and holding me close, he muscled our way out of the store and into the fresh night air, away from the noisy crowd. We sat on the curb. "Put your head down and breathe slowly," he instructed me. He still held me close. A few minutes of silence passed as I slowly but surely got hold of my telepathy. "Feeling better?"

"A little," I said. "Thanks, hon." This wasn't the first time I had lost control of my telepathy. When I first learned I could read the minds of the undead, I spent many a day in pure agony as the thoughts of every single vampire, were folk, and ghost spilled into my brain. Eddie was the one who taught me how to control the mind-reading by focusing on a few minds at a time.

"Do you want to go home?"

I shook my head. "Let's get this blood-tasting thing out of the way."

He got up from the curb. "What store is next on your list?"

I grabbed his outstretched hand. "Trader Drac's."

Trader Drac's was a brand-new store, which had just opened up in the Moonlight Mall, a 24-hour shopping center. The parking lot was almost empty, and Eddie was able to find a spot right next to the main entrance. After spending fifteen minutes attempting to decipher the building's map, we finally (on my insistence) asked the woman vampire at the courtesy desk where Trader Drac's was.

The mall is shaped like a Y, and the store is nestled in the middle. We had parked at the bottom of the letter, causing us to trek up to the middle of the mall. Thankfully, it was a quiet night, and eager kiosk owners, trying to sell everything from overpriced sunglasses to t-shirts with kittens and puppies on them, didn't accost us.

"I like this place, Eddie," I said the second we stepped inside Trader Drac's. Most of the one-room store was lined with cleaned shelves of bottled blood broken down according to the scientific order of the animal kingdom. In the middle of the room, three small couches surrounded a coffee table. I felt I had stepped into a Starbucks for vampires.

Eddie cocked his head as he listened to the music playing over the intercom. "Smooth jazz. A nice change from the last place we visited. I like it." My husband doesn't particularly care for jazz. He's into hard and classic rock, but he was right. The music was nice and very soothing.

A vampire in his early five-hundreds (that's about fifty years for you humans) put down his copy of *Great Expectations* and greeted us with a genuine smile. "Can I help you folks with something?" A nametag reading, Sol, was pinned to his green, cable net sweater, which complemented his grey pleated pants and black penny loafers.

"Yeah," Eddie said. "My wife's a new vampire."

"Say no more," Sol replied. He turned to me. "So, what kinds of blood have you tried?"

"Only swamp rat," I answered.

He shuddered visibly. "I don't know why the hospital gives out that vile liquid. It ruins your palate." He tapped his fingers on his chin in thought. "What are some of your favorite flavors?"

"Well, I like vanilla, strawberry, raspberry, honey, mint—."

"Chocolate," Eddie added.

"But I'm willing to try anything."

Sol smiled. "I like a challenge." He directed us to the couches. "Why don't you and your husband take a seat over there, and I'll put together a tray for you." He looked over at Eddie. "What kind of blood will you be having, sir?"

"I'm good, thank you."-

Sol nodded. "I shall return post-haste!"

Eddie and I sat down on the couch facing Trader Drac's entrance. A thick book titled *Trader Drac's Guide to Your Blood Type* lay on the coffee table. Eddie picked it up and began to thumb through it. "Wow, Shelly! They must have every kind of blood available to vampires." He wrinkled his nose in disgust. "Skunk blood, who drinks that?"

"Why? Does it taste as bad as it smells?" I asked, afraid of the answer. Eddie nodded with a grimace. "Sol," I called "I'm going to pass on any blood that smells bad!"

"I figured you might, so I picked out some blood types which smell divine!" Sol walked over to us, expertly balancing an oval tray containing six wine glasses. Each glass was one-fourth filled with blood. "As you can see, I have labeled the glasses so you can see what kind of blood is in each glass." He set the tray on the table. "Now, the blood that I have selected for you is the most popular. We have sheep, pig, cow, chicken, fruit dragon, and unicorn," he said, pointing to each glass.

I leaned forward and took the sheep's blood. The second I brought the crimson liquid to my lips, I realized Eddie was right. It had a slight coppery taste, but the rest of my taste buds were overrun by a sharp oat sensation. It was as if I had just had eaten a spoonful of dry toasted oats. I love cereal and all, but I certainly didn't want to drink it for the rest of my undead life. I set the glass down in a space I designated to be my "no" pile.

The next choice was pig blood. I'm a big fan of pork, but this one tasted too much like bacon. It went into the no pile.

Cow's blood had a milky taste to it, and so it went into the "maybe" pile. Chicken blood tasted, and, pardon the overused cliché, like chicken. Into the maybe pile, it went. Unicorn blood was next. "This is delicious!" I said the moment it touched my lips.

"What does it taste like?" Eddie asked.

"Apple juice. I might get unicorn blood. Eddie, write it down for me."

My husband reached into his pants pocket and took out a crumpled piece of paper. He took the pen I dug out of my purse and scribbled down "unicorn=apple juice." "Got it, babe."

"The last of this bunch," I said as I sipped the fruit dragon blood. Instantly, my taste buds exploded with a rich yet satisfying flavor. The liquid slid down my throat, giving me a raw power I had never before experienced. I felt I could take on the entire world and win. "Oh. My. God. This is superb!"

Eddie saw my eyes light up in exhilaration. "It must taste

perfect, Shelly." He looked at Sol. "We have a winner. Trust me."

I nodded. "I feel like I just had the ripest, juiciest strawberry dipped in honey."

"How many bottles would you like?" Sol asked as he took out a little pad of paper and a pen from his pants pocket. "I suggest starting off with six twelve-packs priced at six druci a box."

"Well," I hesitated. "Could I try some other kinds just in case I find something else?"

He nodded in agreement. "I'll be right back." He bustled off, leaving us alone.

"Oh, I forgot to tell you. I found the Cloude family. They're alive."

Eddie sighed with relief. He hadn't really been thinking about what happened to the pixie family. He was too preoccupied with my situation. "That's great, Shelly! Are they okay?"

"Kind of. They're staying in one of the flowerbeds at Zephyr Memorial Park."

He sighed, knowing how much I wanted to help the pixie

family. "Shelly, you know they can't come home with us."

"I know, but we have to do something. Maybe the Cloudes could stay with Robin."

Eddie gave a small laugh. "Yes, have them stay with your brother, who controls plants with his mind."

"Okay, bad idea," I admitted. "Do you have any ideas?"

He shook his head. "You're the brains of this marriage."

"And you're the brawn?"

"You got that right, babe!" he said, playfully flexing both biceps. I have seen those muscles up close and personal, and believe me, there is no flab anywhere. He stopped flexing and became serious. "We'll think of something, even if it means renting a place with our own backyard."

"Which we wouldn't be able to afford if I get laid off," I reminded him.

"Then, I'll work extra hours at the diner."

"Don't do that. You'll just get overtired and cranky."

"I'm never cranky!"

I rolled my eyes at him. "The week we got back from our honeymoon, you worked three double shifts in a row on just three hours of sleep," I reminded him.

"Oh, yeah," he said as his ego deflated. "I could barely keep my eyes open at that time."

Sol came back with another tray filled with five more glasses of blood, and our conversation came to a halt. He told us what they were and gave the prices, which were pretty steep compared to the other kinds.

Bear blood had a beef jerky taste to it. Crocodile blood was incredibly salty. When I drank the elephant blood, I felt like I had stuffed my mouth full of those nasty, door stopper marshmallow circus peanuts. The lightly salted shark blood was fine at first but had a very gritty aftertaste. Fire dragon blood nearly scorched the roof of my mouth with its lava hot taste. Fortunately, it was the last one.

Sol looked at me with anticipation. "Have you made your final decision yet?" he asked me.

I managed a nod as my throat felt like it was on fire. "Yeah," I rasped, "I'm sticking with the fruit dragon blood."

"Excellent choice. How many boxes will you be buying?"

Eddie and I looked at each other for a moment. "We'll go

with your recommendation," I finally said.

Minutes later, we were lugging six boxes of fruit dragon blood out to the car. Eddie had to set his three boxes on the hood of the car so he could retrieve the car keys from his pants pocket. After unlocking the door, we carefully placed the boxes in the backseat. I winced every time I heard the glass bottles clink against each other. "Drive slowly, Eddie," I told him. Before my husband became a vampire at the age of twenty-five, he raced cars to pay for his college education. Even after forty some odd years, he still has a lead foot.

"I will," he promised me with a kiss as we got in the car.

I glanced back at the bottles and considered, for a moment, buckling them in, too. "We still haven't got a gift for Bruce and Libby."

"We've got plenty of time," Eddie said as he started the car and began to back up.

"No, we don't. The wedding's tomorrow."

He let out a small groan as he shifted gears. "And at one in the afternoon!" Getting up six hours earlier than usual was definitely not his cup of tea.

"Never fear, I have figured out the perfect gift for them!"

"And that is?"

"A gift card from Bed and Bath Emporium. I was thinking about setting a twenty-five druci limit."

"That's a great idea, babe, but there's just one tiny flaw in your plan. The Bed and Bath Emporium is closed."

"You see, hon, that's the beauty of gift cards. You can buy them anywhere, and I know that Syntax Drugs is open 24/7."

"But do they have the gift card?"

"Yes, they do. Plus, we can pick up some food before paying the Cloudes a quick visit."

"Excellent idea. To Syntax Drugs, it is then!"

After getting the gift card and some food for the pixie family, we drove to Zephyr Memorial Park. It was Eddie who spotted Eva, one of the twenty pixie children, darting back and forth from their shabby little three-level house, pieced crudely together from bark, twigs, and leaves. We waved to her, and she called shrilly, "Mom, Shelly and Eddie are here!"

Addison flew out the front door, followed by three of her

daughters, Raine, Maxie, and Sharona. "Quiet, Eva, or you'll wake the rest of your brothers and sisters!" She looked at us with weary eyes. "Hello, you two!"

Eddie and I sat cross-legged on the grass. "We brought you some food," I said as I spilled the contents of a plastic shopping bag on the ground. "Six fruit cups, two packages of dried fruit, and six candy bars."

"Thank you," Addison said. She and her daughters collected the food and took it into their temporary home. Then she came back out.

"Is there anything else we can do for you?" I asked.

"A more permanent home would be nice," the pixie matriarch said wistfully.

"We're working on that," Eddie assured her.

"We're having difficulty keeping away some raccoons who have been attacking our house."

Out of the corner of my eye, I saw movement in the bushes behind us. I turned halfway around to see what it was. A masked face peeked out and gave a low growl towards the flowerbeds. A short but loud cougar-like scream suddenly filled the night air, and the raccoon high-tailed it out of there. I turned back to see my husband and the pixies staring in shock at me. I suddenly clamped my hand over my mouth. That sound had come from my lips.

"I don't think you'll be having any problems with raccoons tonight," Eddie told Addison. He took my hand as he sent me a telepathic message. *I don't know what just happened, but I'm so turned on right now.*

I nodded in agreement. Raw, sensual power was sweeping through my entire body. *Me, too. We need to get home.* "Uh, Addison," I said, trying to control myself. "Are you guys all set?"

Addison smiled with a knowing wink. "We're fine. Go on, you two."

Chapter Five:
Why Dinosaurs Aren't Invited To Weddings

I open my eyes and see murky water all around me.

There is a young girl who has been pushed out of a boat by her

sister. She is struggling to swim to the surface. I reach out to

grab her, but I can't. My eyes drift upwards as a watery, familiar

face appears just above the surface. It's my father. He grabs the

girl by the collar of her shirt and yanks her out of the water. She

turns to me, and to my horror, I see a younger version of myself.

I woke up with a gasp from the terrifying dream, forgetting

momentarily where I was. I sat up in bed and glanced over at my

sleeping husband. I lay back on my pillow as I thought about this

latest dream.

It wasn't the first time I have had it. I remember when I

was little, I would wake up screaming in fear. The dream always felt real, and in the back of my mind, I knew it had happened to me at one point in my life. Dad or Mom would run into my room and calm me down, but when I would tell them the dream and how real it was, they would assure me that it was only a dream, and nobody had ever tried to drown me.

I glanced at the alarm clock. We had an hour before getting ready for Bruce and Libby's wedding. No sense in waking up, Eddie. I shut my eyes and forced myself to fall back asleep. This time there was no dream.

The odd dream was still on my mind as Eddie and I showered and got ready for the wedding. I hadn't even told my husband about it because it was only "a silly dream," as my mother had always told me. I stood in front of the closet outside the bedroom, debating on what to wear.

Eddie came out of our room wearing a white short-sleeve shirt tucked into a pair of black dress pants. He held up two ties in his hands. "Which one do you like? The blue or orange one?"

"Blue's fine, honey," I said, distractedly.

He put his arms around me. "Are you all right, babe?"

"Oh, I'm fine. I was just thinking about a dream I had last night."

He frowned. "Another nightmare about the attack?"

I shook my head as I made my decision and grabbed a dark purple sleeveless shirt and a pair of black dress slacks. "No, just a recurring one I've had since growing up."

He followed me into our room and sat on the edge of the bed while he put on his tie. "Want to talk about it?" he asked.

I shrugged out of my bathrobe and put on my outfit while I told him my dream. He didn't say a word but listened to me intently. "So, what do you make of it?" I finally asked.

He looked up from slipping on his black socks and dress shoes. "Let me get this straight. You've had this dream since you were little?"

"Well, different versions of it," I answered, sitting next to him and putting on my black dress sandals.

"And the little girl is really you?"

"Yeah, but I don't remember almost drowning."

"Well, it could have happened when you were really little, like two or three. That could be why you don't remember it."

"I don't think so. Because in the dream I'm seven or eight. And I clearly would have remembered someone trying to drown me."

"But your parents told you it never happened, right?"

"I know it happened," I said as I got a pretty turquoise stone trio on a delicate silver chain from my jewelry box. "Could you help me with this?"

"Shelly," Eddie said as he fastened my necklace, "you have a great memory. Don't get me wrong, but is there any chance you could've seen something similar? Maybe you saw someone get pushed out of a boat."

"No! I know my sister pushed me out of a boat."

"But, I thought Robin was your only sibling."

"He is, but that's the thing. Always in this dream, my sister, whom I don't have, is trying to drown me. That's not the only dream where she has tried to kill me."

"Really?"

"Yeah, I've been pushed down a flight of stairs in some versions. I've been shoved in front of a moving car. I've been stabbed with a steak knife. It's always the same little girl. But last night's dream confirmed in the back of my mind that this kid was my sister."

"That you've never had."

"Exactly!"

"Maybe you did have a sister, but she died at birth or something."

I shook my head vehemently. "No. I've asked on several occasions if I ever had a sister, and my parents both said it has always been just Robin and me. Even when my mom died, there was no mention of another sibling."

All this talking was making me thirsty, so we walked into the kitchen. I grabbed a bottle of fruit dragon blood out of the refrigerator. I drank about a third of it. "Do you think I've consumed my blood intake for the day?"

"Probably," Eddie said as he slipped on his suit coat. "Do you have the gift?"

I nodded as I put the chilled blood back in the fridge. "It's in my purse. Ow!" I said, covering my mouth with my hand.

"You okay?" he asked as he popped open an umbrella to keep the dangerous sunlight off me.

"Yeah, I just cut my tongue on my fangs again. That really hurts."

"Good thing we heal fast."

"I know," I said, as I could feel the cut and pain disappear, "because if we didn't, I'd have no tongue." I put my shield bracelet over my left arm and snapped it shut. I grabbed my purse and looked at the time on my cell phone. "Oh, crap! We're going to be late. We've got to leave now."

"What did Mr. Miller say to you?"

I sighed. "It was before the attack. Bruce told me Libby was really stressed out and didn't want me to ruin anything."

Eddie grunted. "What is his problem this time?"

"He told me trouble always follows me, and I have a destructive nature. So, I'm supposed to be on my best behavior today."

Eddie's eyes narrowed angrily. "What a bunch of frigging bull crap! Trouble does follow you, but you're certainly not destructive."

"He cited several occasions where I've put someone in danger."

"Don't tell me he brought up the book demon again! You saved the city from that thing." He nearly yanked the door off its hinges in frustration. "One of these days, that jerk's going to go too far, and I won't be able to control myself."

"Eddie," I said with a pleading sigh, "can we just drop the subject and go?" The last thing I wanted was my husband to go "all Hulk" on Bruce. I followed Eddie out the door with him holding the umbrella over my head.

We arrived at Eden Gardens Hotel with minutes to spare and were led to the largest conference room they had. It was decked out in hunter green and blue striped wallpaper and blue carpet. Almost all of the 300 hunter green padded chairs were filled with people. Eddie and I chose two seats in the back row that faced the raised platform decorated with soft pink roses and baby's breath. The bridesmaid dresses were all ruffles and bows in pink. Even my dad, Timothy Anderson, the best man, was wearing an ugly pink cummerbund. Saying that Libby loved pink was a complete understatement. Other than my dad and the wedding couple, the only other people I recognized in the wedding party were my stepmother, Amelia, who was the maid of honor, and my sister-in-law, Lisa, and her brother, Roger. From what Lisa had told me, the rest of the twelve-member party were friends and relatives of Libby's.

The wedding march began to play, and the congregation stood up as the elfin bride was led down the aisle by her oldest son, Darren. She wore a sleeveless off-white dress that reached the floor. A four-foot-long train trailed behind her. She had let her blond hair grow out past her shoulders and now had it swept into an elaborate bun with two long tendrils. Her purple eyes were focused on the stage and Bruce.

Once the music stopped, we all sat down, and the ceremony began. An hour and a half later, we were still at the ceremony. Eddie telepathically said to me after checking his watch, *This is the longest wedding I've ever been to.*

I nodded. The ceremony was beautiful but incredibly long. The first half had your usual songs and readings, but Libby had asked the officiant, an elfin priest in his eighties, to read the vows in old Elfish and in English. *I know*, I told Eddie, and *I have to go to the bathroom. But I don't want to leave and be presumed rude.*

It looks like it's wrapping up. I'm so glad we kept our ceremony only a half-hour long.

"I now pronounce you, man and wife. You may kiss the bride," said the priest. Both Bruce and Libby kissed for almost two minutes.

Come on, come on! I thought to myself. *Say, "Ladies and gentlemen, I present to you the loving couple Mr. and Mrs.............."*

The priest said the magic words, and the wedding finally ended. I made a beeline for the nearest bathroom.

When I came out, Eddie was waiting for me. "Feeling better?" he asked with a grin.

"Yes, much better," I replied as I took his hand. "I hope there's coffee at the reception because I really need it."

A satyr with a brown goatee carrying a silver tray crashed into me. The hors d'oeuvres clattered to the ground. "I'm so sorry," he said as he knelt down to clean up the mess.

I bent down and began to help pick up the remaining food. "It's okay. Don't worry about it."

The balding satyr who was dressed in your typical caterer's outfit looked up at me with intense brown eyes. "You're alive!" He backed away slowly and gave me a slight bow before disappearing into the kitchen nearby.

"That was weird," I said to Eddie as we exchanged puzzled looks. "Did he just bow to me?"

Eddie nodded in shocked agreement. "I think he did, and you know what? He's the satyr I saw with the one-eyed vampire yesterday."

"Coincidence," I said, but we both didn't believe it.

The food, a vegan menu, wasn't too bad, except for the nasty coffee. Eddie and I sat at a table with one of Libby's incredibly snooty relatives who identified himself as Uncle Larry. He kept slapping the butt of the raven-haired werewolf who was filling our water glasses. Even though she was in her human form, I could still read parts of her mind, and she was not happy with the situation.

"I really don't think she wants her butt slapped by a drunken stranger," I said after choking down a gulp of the coffee.

Nasty or not, I really needed the caffeine jolt.

Uncle Larry brushed me off. "What you don't understand is that these poor people really need to be happy." He gave Eddie a conspiratorial wink. "And the ladies love it. I bet your wife wouldn't mind."

"If you slapped Shelly on the butt, she would rip your arm off and beat you senseless with it," Eddie looked at me. "Isn't that right, dear?"

"Most likely. Larry, I strongly advise that you not to slap the waitress again."

Uncle Larry snorted. "She's a woman. What's she going to do?" The server came by again, and Uncle Larry gave her another "love pat" on the rump. Big mistake.

A dark-skinned hand shot out at the drunken elf's throat, and she lifted him effortlessly out of his chair. Her other hand grabbed at the air, and suddenly, a small dagger appeared. She placed the blade at the man's throat and stared at him with deadly dark eyes. "What shall I do to him? Gut or slice?" She was directing the question to me.

Our table sat silent, but inwardly, Eddie and I were slightly amused. "Are you talking to me?" I asked.

"Yes," she answered. Her watchful eyes never left Uncle Larry. "What do you want me to do with this vermin?"

"Well," I said, looking at the stain on Uncle Larry's pants, "I think he's learned his lesson. You should put him down and not injure him." I really hoped she'd listen to me.

She nodded and let go of him. He dropped to the floor, breathing heavily. "Don't touch me again," she warned Uncle Larry. She made a sweeping motion with her hand, and the dagger vanished. Before leaving the table, she gave me a slight bow.

Now, werefolks minds are hard to read when in their human form, but I got a snippet of her mind. She thought I was someone very important, but I couldn't read anymore because I was aware that the room had become suddenly quiet as everyone stared at me.

"Whoa," Eddie whispered to me, breaking the silence. "This is awkward."

"What did I do?" I whispered to him, completely baffled.

"You just saved Uncle Larry from being gutted."

"I know that, but why are Bruce and Libby glaring at me? Shouldn't they be happy I adverted bloodshed?"

"I don't know."

The reception dragged on for another two hours, and I was on my fifth glass of sparkling cider. Most of the guests had left, leaving the ballroom almost empty. I reached for my drink, but I guess I still had my clumsy nature and dumped my cider onto the tablecloth and into my lap. Super. "I'm going to the bathroom to wipe this stuff off," I told Eddie. Without letting my husband respond, I sprinted to the nearest bathroom.

I shut the door behind me and leaned towards the sink. Grabbing a handful of useless non-absorbent napkins from the wall-mounted dispenser, I started to dab at the massive stain on the front of my shirt. Unfortunately, I had gotten the brunt of the spill. This day was snowballing into a hellish descent. Then it got worse. Much worse.

I looked up into the mirror, and my body turned into pudding at what I saw. A yellow reptilian eye peered out at me through the crack in the stall door closest to the exit. My breath caught in my throat as my eyes carefully scanned under the stall door. A large, sharp hook claw protruded from the second toe of two reptilian legs. I had seen claws like that before. Of course, that was in a movie. *Oh, crap! Oh, crap! Oh, crap! Oh, crap!* I said to myself. *There's a velociraptor in the bathroom! How did a creature who has been extinct for millions of years end up in a four-star motel bathroom? Snap out of Shelly,* I reprimanded myself. *Who cares about that right now? The more pressing question is, how do I get out of here in one piece?*

Time stood still for only a few moments as I quickly weighed my escape options. The bathroom door was out of the question. Even though I'm twice as fast as the average human (thanks to my new vampire skills,) I knew the raptor in its current position would have the advantage. No windows meant no getaway.

My eyes focused on the removable tiles ceiling. Air ducts. "Well," I said under my breath, "if it worked in Jurassic Park, it could work for me." I jumped straight up. When I neared the ceiling, I did an impressive somersault and kicked at some of the tiles, creating a hole big enough for me to fit through. Plaster cascaded around me as I fell back down onto the linoleum floor, landing on my feet like a cat and completely unscathed.

The velociraptor chose that moment to send the stall door flying off its hinges with a powerful kick. The door crashed into the wall with a loud BANG! Then the creature emerged. It was a genuinely frightening, brown lizard, towering over me nearly seven feet as it stood on its hind legs. It charged in my direction, giving a loud, gurgling roar.

"Time to move!" I said to myself as I jumped straight up for the hole in the ceiling. Reaching the top, I grabbed the ragged edges of plaster and metal and hoisted myself up into the ceiling. The raptor lept up at me, and when its head and snapping jaws just cleared the hole, I kicked its jaw as hard as I could. It fell to the ground with a whimper and was still. I peered cautiously out of the hole. Its chest was moving up and down slowly. Crap. I had only stunned it. I sat back in the claustrophobic air shaft.

I now had a major quandary on my hands with only two options. I could jump back down the hole and escape through a normal exit, such as the door, or I could crawl through the ceiling until I reached another room far away from the dinosaur. There was a very slim chance of surviving the first option since the raptor was directly below me. If I drastically miscalculated the jump, I'd end up looking like I had been through a paper shredder.

"Option two it is." I began crawling as fast as I could on top of the dropped ceiling tiles as they crumbled away behind me. Okay, definitely not making a quiet retreat. I made for the bathroom door as my first destination. Finally, I found my footing on something solid. I was evidently out of the bathroom. I paused for a moment. While on my journey through the ceiling tiles, I'd encountered several cobweb strands with my face. I quickly wiped them away as I made a mental map of my location. The reception hall was the last room on the left, and that's where my final destination was.

I was amazed at how well my vampire eyesight was kicking in. I could see everything clearly, but it was like looking through a pair of binoculars. I began speed crawling again towards the music and the voices coming from the reception hall.

Fifty cobwebs and twenty empty rodent nests later, I found myself crawling on some more dropped ceiling tiles. I hadn't gone too far when they crumbled under my weight, and I found myself plummeting to the floor. You could have heard a pin drop when I made my unconventional entrance.

Bruce pushed himself away from his table and stormed up to me. "What do you think you're doing?" he growled in a low whisper.

"Everyone needs to leave now!" I told him.

He grabbed my wrist and yanked me off the ground. "No, I will not have you ruin my wedding day." He looked at me disdainfully. "Geesh, look at you. You can't even make yourself presentable."

"Let go of my wife!" Eddie ordered Bruce. My husband had seen me fall and ran over to make sure I was okay but was now really ticked off at the groom. Bruce let go of me. "You okay, Shelly?" my husband asked.

I nodded and then said in a loud voice. "Everyone needs to leave now!" Murmurs of "Why?" echoed across the room.

"Because there's a velociraptor in the women's bathroom!"

"How dare you make up such a vicious lie on my wedding day?" Libby screamed at me.

"I'm not lying!" I said.

As if to prove my point, the dinosaur came crashing through the main doors. It quickly picked me out of the dwindling crowd, probably because I was the only one covered from head to toe in plaster dust and cobwebs. It jumped at me with its sharp meat-tearing talons extended.

"Citadel!" Eddie cried as he stepped in front of me. A green force field instantly appeared between us and the raptor, but the momentum of the reptile's leap knocked us off our feet. Unfortunately, my husband lost concentration, and the spell dissipated.

"Move!" I ordered Eddie as a lethal claw swung out at our heads. We both rolled away in opposite directions. Screams filled the reception hall as the remaining crowd fled the scene. I was starting to feel abandonment issues when I realized Eddie and I were the only people left in the room.

"Shelly, catch!" Eddie said as he tossed me Knowledge in its book form. Then he threw his palms outward and shouted, "Nebulae!" Two white, hot fireballs shot out from his hands and hurled towards the dinosaur. The spell did little damage to the raptor. It only squealed in pain as if it had touched a hot burner. Eddie took this tiny window of opportunity to run to my side.

"Knowledge is power!" I said the second, my fingers touched the book jacket. Green sparks flew around the book as it changed into a sheathed sword. I expertly hoisted the empty scabbard on my back. I touched a small button on the underside of my bracelet and activated the shield before withdrawing Knowledge. "How does that old saying go? ' The couple that fights together—.' "

"Doesn't get eaten by a dinosaur?" Eddie finished as he fell to one knee and retrieved his Scorpion XL, a high-powered handgun that fires laser bullets, from his ankle holster. He got up quickly and fired three quick shots at Barney the Dinosaur, who was charging full speed at us. "Crap!" he shouted as the bullets only gave the living fossil flesh wounds. "This thing's got one tough hide."

I slashed at the creature with my sword and chopped off one of its paws. Apparently, the hide was weak when it came to magical swords. It roared in pain and backed away. "I think it's retreating!" I was wrong. With blood dripping off its severed stump, it snarled as it prepared to take us down with a flying leap.

"Nope! I'm pretty sure you ticked it off," Eddie said as he fired two more ineffective bullets. "We've got to think of something fast. I've got one more bullet left in the chamber."

"You didn't bring any extra clips with you?"

"Fighting a velociraptor wasn't on my agenda today."

An idea popped into my head. "I've got a plan."

"Is this one of your crazy plans that could either get us killed or miraculously save us?"

"Yes."

"Okay, what is it?"

"You distract it while I sneak up behind the dinosaur and chop its head off."

"Sounds like a plan," He gave me a quick kiss. "Be careful."

"I will."

"Hey, Littlefoot!" Eddie shouted at the oversized lizard as he held up his gun-free hand. "Duracell!" he said as a blue, beach ball-sized sphere of pure energy began hovering over his open palm. He smirked as the dino's eyes were glued on the energy ball. "Ooh, you like this, don't you?" He casually tossed the ball towards the ceiling.

While he was keeping the raptor busy, I stealthily slipped around to its left side. Then I quickly backed up a few steps before I made a running leap. While I was in mid-air and directly over the dinosaur's neck, I sliced off its head with one swift sweep of Knowledge. It slumped to the ground, lifeless, while I landed in a crouch on the thin carpet. I wiped off the blood on the creature's hide before putting my sword back in its sheath.

"Way to go, babe!" Eddie said as he came rushing over to me.

"Excellent Land Before Time reference, honey!" I said as we high-fived each other. Then I noticed something on the back of one of the raptor's legs. It looked like a tattoo with writing on it. I gave a shocked gasp. There was the blue lion with the three fleurs-de-lis and the inscription, "Property of Queen Rachel."

Eddie peeked over my shoulder to see why I was so dumbfounded. "That's the emblem on your shield," he said quietly.

I nodded, not taking my eyes off the tattoo. "And the name? This can't be a coincidence!"

"Look at what you did!" Libby screamed as she and Bruce stormed out of the kitchen where they and the rest of the wedding party had taken cover. "You harpy!" She pointed a gloved hand at me. "You ruined my wedding!"

I reeled back in shock. My ears refused to believe what I was hearing.

"Shelly just saved your lives," Eddie pointed out as his blood began to boil with anger. "You should at least be a little grateful."

"Libby," Bruce growled as he stepped forward, "let me handle this." He glared at me with angry green eyes. "Look at what you've done, Shelly! You've trashed this place."

"But—but," I stammered, "I didn't mean to. I was trying to—." I shot pleading glances at my father, my stepmother, and anyone else. My heart broke in two, and I couldn't tell if it was from the shock at the treatment I was receiving or the fact the only person defending me was my husband.

"Shut up!" Bruce screamed. "You think you're some kind

of hero? Well, let me tell you the real truth, Shelly. You are a stupid, irresponsible cow!"

That's when Eddie lost it. No more Mr. Nice Vampire. Before anyone could stop him, he drew back one of his fists and popped Bruce in the mouth, sending the ex-cop staggering backward. "Don't ever talk to Shelly like that again! Apologize to her!"

Bruce touched his newly split lip as sparks began to dance on his fingertips. Then using his electrokinesis, the red and gray-haired groom threw a bolt of electricity at Eddie. "You son of a whore!" he screamed.

Eddie dodged out of the way and prepared an energy spell to throw at Bruce when Dad stepped in between them. "Stop it, both of you, before you kill somebody! Eddie, calm down. Bruce is kind of stressed right now."

My jaw dropped in horror as Dad stuck up for Bruce the dirtbag. Tears began to fill my eyes. "What the frig, Dad?" The plea came out hoarse as a basketball-size lump formed in my throat. I ran over to the broken table where Eddie and I had been sitting, grabbed my belongings, and stormed out. I had a strong feeling Eddie and I weren't going to be receiving a thank-you note.

Chapter Six:
I Receive a Mysterious Plea for Help

I curled up in a fetal position on the couch in the living room. My body shook as I fought to control the tears of anger and hurt flowing out of me. The only consolation was my husband's arms around me.

"How dare Bruce say those things to me?" I said to him. "How was I supposed to know that a carnivorous dinosaur was lurking in the women's bathroom." The real hurt was my father not standing up for me.

"They're all a bunch of ungrateful losers," Eddie said. "You risked your life to warn them."

"They leave us in danger, and then yell at us after we kill the thing!" I grunted.

"We should have just left them and not saved their sorry hides," Eddie said. He excused himself to use the bathroom.

And what was going on with me? I had been nearly killed three times in less than a month! First, the vampire, then the robots, and now a velociraptor? Who had I angered so much they wanted me dead? I looked up from my pity party to hear pounding on the front door. After listening for a moment, I determined it wasn't knocking, but someone hammering something on the front door.

Peeking out at the front, I saw the side profile of our landlord tacking up a piece of paper to the siding. "Good God, what is he trying to do? Nail his 95 theses to the door?" I grumbled as I pulled myself together and wiped the remaining tears out of my eyes.

Storming out from the kitchen, I swung open the front door to confront Vinnie. "What the frig is wrong with you?" I snarled. "Do you want to crack the siding?"

The satyr gave me a slimy smile as he tore off a piece of the paper he had just nailed to the house and handed it to me. "Your eviction notice. I want you out by the end of the month."

I stared down at the piece of paper and shook my head in disgusted disbelief. "On what grounds?"

"For killing Poopsie!"

A smile crossed my face. Well, that's one bright spot in my day. "Someone killed Poopsie?" I asked, pleasantly surprised.

"Oh, don't be so surprised!" Vinnie snapped, "I can see the guilt written all over your face. You wanted that sweet puppy dead, and you or Eddie put a bullet in each one of that poor hellhound's heads."

"Vinnie, I can assure you that Eddie and I had nothing to do with Poopsie's untimely death." But I would like to shake the person's hand who did. "You can't go around accusing people of something they didn't do."

"No, but I can evict them," he turned away. "Remember, you're out by the end of the month." Then the scumbag left me standing in the front door with our eviction notice in my trembling hand.

When my husband came back to the living room, I told him the bad news. "Vinnie's doing what?" Eddie shouted angrily, "That has to be illegal! I'm going over there and—."

"Eddie," I said as I began to rub my temples. Vampires can't get migraines, but there's a first time for everything. "Don't get into another fight."

"But, Shelly, he's accused us of killing that blasted hellhound!"

"And if you decide to punch Vinnie's lights out—which he fully deserves, by the way—it'll only confirm his off-the-wall suspicions. Plus, he'll have you arrested for assault."

Eddie shrugged his shoulders to loosen the building tension and gave a reluctant sigh. "Good point."

Tears began of frustration started to flow down my cheeks again. "I'm so tired of crappy things dumped on me these past month."

"I know, I know." Eddie hugged me tightly. "We'll get through this together, babe. We always do."

I sighed heavily as I leaned my head against him. "What do you suggest?" I asked quietly.

"First, we should take a nap and clear our heads. Then we put together a reasonable plan to take on Vinnie."

I gave a tired smile. "Or maybe a miracle will bring us out

of our new financial woes."

Naps do wondrous things. Not only do they help clear your head, but also they help you forget your troubles momentarily. We lay awake in bed, not wanting to get out from under the warm blankets. "Did I tell you how awesome you were when you killed that dinosaur?" Eddie asked me quietly as total adoration filled his green eyes.

I smiled at him. "Are you saying decapitation turns you on?"

He gave a small laugh. "No, but the way you handled your sword, it was so precise. You took total control of the situation and completely kept your cool. I felt like I was watching a seasoned warrior queen with a super-hot body."

"Thanks, but maybe Bruce was right. I feel like I'm somehow responsible for letting that raptor in the hotel."

"Shelly, don't say things like that. Bruce is a jerk, and he had no right to say those things to you."

"Thanks for sticking up for me back there, Eddie. I felt like you were my only ally." Tears began to fill my eyes as the hurtful words came back to my mind. "I still can't believe what he called me!"

Eddie pulled me close to him and hugged me tightly. "I'm so sorry, Shell." He paused and then gave a grin. "It sure felt good when I clobbered him."

I wiped away the tears as I lay on his chest. "I bet it did." We were silent for a long time until I finally spoke. "I suppose we should get up now."

"Probably," he said as we both rolled out of bed. "Plus, I'm starving. How about you?" He pulled on a pair of blue jeans and a dark green Rolling Stones t-shirt.

I slipped off my purple shirt, which was spotted with dried dinosaur blood and put on a pink and green vertically striped, long-sleeved tee, blue jeans, and socks. "Me, too. Plus, I'm really thirsty," I said as we padded into the kitchen.

"For blood?"

I had a sudden idea. "I wonder how fruit dragon blood would taste if it were in an ice cream float," I said as I opened the fridge door and unscrewed a bottle of blood. I took a swig. The sweet liquid flowed down my throat, quenching my thirst.

"Probably pretty good," Eddie replied as he bent down to pick up an envelope off the floor by the front door. "Hey, did you drop a piece of mail?"

I put the bottle back and went over to him. "No. Why?"

"Where did this come from?"

We both stared at the envelope addressed to Mrs. Michelle Van Helsing in elegant handwriting. The paper itself was cream colored and had an expensive look to it. "Well, let's open it and see what's inside."

He turned the envelope over and gasped at the seal. It was the exact emblem as on my shield. "What the?" Then he slowly opened it up and took out a folded piece of paper. It read: "Mrs. Michelle Van Helsing, we need your help! Some of us knew your mother, Sara Marie, when she was a little girl, and we know that she would have wanted you to help us. May she rest in peace. Please meet us tonight at the Scurvy Motel at eight o'clock." The writing was an exact match to the outside of the envelope.

My whole body began to tremble. Who would know about my mother? I frantically searched the paper for a signature, but there was none. "Who wrote this?" I nearly shouted.

 "I have no idea. Shelly, calm down."

"I can't! Who are these people, and how do they know my mother?"

He put his hands on my shoulders and looked at me squarely in the eyes. "It's going to be okay." He motioned me to sit down at the kitchen table as he sat across from me. "Let's talk about this. I thought your family's first time here was over six years ago."

"It was the first time. Believe me, I would've remembered coming to this reality growing up."

He looked over the letter carefully. "What do you know about your mother?"

"What do you mean? You're talking about my own mother!"

"Shelly, just tell me."

I swallowed hard. "Well, you know she died when I was thirteen."

"Car accident, right?"

I nodded. "Mom and Dad married right after college. They

had Robin and then me. She played the piano and homeschooled us. She was a really wonderful mother." Tears began to form in my eyes as I wiped them away with the heel of my hand.

"Wish I could've met her," Eddie said softly.

"She would've loved you."

"Most people do," he said with a grin that cheered me up a little. "So, was her name really Sara Marie?"

"Well, Marie was her middle name."

"These people mentioned they knew your mom when she was a little girl."

"That's impossible!" I said. "Grandpa and Grandma O'Malley died in a plane crash in the Amazon rainforest when Mom was seven. She was the only survivor." I paused as I thought for a moment. Had they died in the rainforests of Brazil or in the Himalayas? I seriously couldn't remember where their plane had crashed. I shut my eyes and stretched into the recesses of my memories to figure out what Mom had told me about her parents. Stilled pictures of my life flitted through my mind until I gasped aloud on one particular image.

"Are you all right?" Eddie asked, gently touching my wrist.

"Yeah, I think so. I just remembered something. When David first gave me the shield, I knew I had seen that symbol somewhere before."

"Did you just figure it out?"

I nodded. "When I was a kid, I used to sneak around the house, hunting for possible Christmas presents. One time—I must have been eight or nine—I was snooping around my parents' bedroom closet, and I came across this plaque with three fleurs-de-lis surrounding a blue lion."

"Like your shield?"

"Exactly like my shield! Mom caught me, and when I asked her about the plaque, she told me it was her family coat of arms."

He saw me looking at my watch. It was almost seven. "You aren't seriously considering going to meet these people, are you?"

"Yeah," I said hesitantly. "Well, it sounds like someone really needs my help."

"It could be a trap."

"Oh, I hadn't thought of that." But something in my gut told me that I should go. "But what if it isn't? I have to know what's going on. This is my mother we're talking about."

Eddie gave a sigh of reluctance. "Okay, but I'm going with you."

"Oh, definitely! I wouldn't go down there by myself in broad daylight." Scurvy Motel was a really sketchy motel where 99% of their clientele were either drug dealers or prostitutes. The worst part? The contractors had built it down by the wrong side of the docks.

"Then we better equip ourselves," Eddie said as he disappeared into the bedroom. Moments later, he came back into the kitchen carrying the black and silver nylon ninja utility belt I had given him as a wedding gift and a small duffle bag. He set both items on the table and unzipped the duffle bag.

I peered into the bag. "How come you never use these?" I asked as I picked up a wooden throwing star with retractable, deadly blades. There were three others: a wooden one and two silver ones.

"Actually, I forget they're there most of the time," he said as he began transferring the three silver throwing knives, the three wooden stakes, and the rest of the throwing stars into the various durable nylon compartments.

I handed him back the throwing star. "You should use these weapons more often instead of your spells. That way, you can reserve your strength." I put my shield bracelet on my left wrist and put on my sneakers.

He took out another Scorpion XL in a hip holster and looped it through the strap on the utility belt. "I'll probably use these weapons more now that I have better access to them. Ready to go?"

"Almost," I said as I took Knowledge in her book form off the kitchen table. "Knowledge is power." I delivered the incantation in a resolute, confident voice as my hand lay flat on the cover. Green sparks flew around my hand as the book morphed into my trusty sword. I slung the sheath over my back and tightened the straps. "Now, I'm ready." I turned to face my husband.

The ride to the docks was quiet, except for the roar of

Eddie's motorcycle. I wrapped my arms around my vampire's

waist as we sped across town. I could feel the wind hitting my

sheath against my helmet. That didn't bother me because I was

thinking about the mysterious letter and the reference to my

mother.

The whole thing was puzzling and very scary at the same

time. Mom couldn't have known anyone in this dimension. I was

almost positive that Dad would've mentioned it to my brother or

me. Then my mind wandered back to the conversation about my

mom. All I really knew about her past was that she was

orphaned at the age of eight. That was it. What really puzzled

me was her supposed "coat of arms." David had said the very

same symbols belonged to a line of ancient, royal warriors from

this realm, not mine.

We arrived at the hotel fifteen minutes early. Eddie parked

the bike in the parking lot, and we walked into the disgusting

lobby. Painted giant neon arrows streaked back and forth across

the red walls. A fifteen or sixteen-year-old Goth fairy with a nose

ring was sitting behind the bright green desk. He wore a white t-shirt under his black leather jacket. When he got up, I could hear the squeaking of his tight, leather pants. Even his black feather antennae and black wings were going for the whole Goth look as well. He peered out at us from under his long, black bangs. "Sweet sword!" he said.

"Thanks," I replied.

"You guys want a room?"

"No!" I answered hastily. God, I didn't even want to think about the condition of the room. "We're meeting someone here."

"Ooh, kinky!"

"Look, kid," Eddie said, trying his hardest not to roll his eyes, "if someone comes looking for us, tell them we'll be sitting over there." He nodded to a small waiting area with a coffee table that screamed for a new paint job and three rainbow-colored, faux leather couches. I could feel my eyes burning from the sight of them. The one consolation was the coffee maker percolating on a nearby counter. After removing Knowledge from my back, I sat down on one of the couches and laid the sword across my lap.

"Want some coffee?" my husband asked me.

"Sure, hon."

He walked over, grabbed two Styrofoam cups, and filled them up with coffee, cream, and sugar. The second he brought the coffee to his lips, he spewed the liquid back in the cup. "This is worse than gas station coffee!" He handed me my cup.

Peering into the cup, I took a tentative sniff of the so-called "coffee." It smelled okay, but the taste was a different story. "Blech! You're right, Eddie. This is the nastiest coffee I've ever had."

"Well, I can assure you that the *Monte Carlo* has the finest coffee you've ever tasted, your Highness."

Eddie and I both turned to face a barrel-chested, six-foot vampire dressed in an open black leather, 1940's panzer jacket over a crisp, white dress shirt and black tie. The shirt was tucked neatly into a pair of pressed black slacks with a thick red stripe running down the outside of each leg. A red beret with a blue lion surrounded by three fleurs-de-lis sat upon his black, military-style hair. I could see only one of his gray eyes because a black eye patch covered up the right one. I couldn't tell his age, but I pegged him to be in his two-hundreds.

He wasn't the only one who had entered the lobby. On his right was the werewolf who had nearly killed Uncle Larry. She was in her werewolf form and dressed in full desert fatigues and black combat boots.

Another werewolf stood next to her. His dark eyes gave us the once over and nodded in approval. "She's the one, Cassius," he said to the vampire, "and her Guardian, I can tell, is incredibly protective of her," he said in a gruff voice.

It was then I realized Eddie had moved in front of me, just in case these people decided to try anything funny. I got up from the couch and placed my hand on the sword's hilt. "Who are you?" I asked.

"Your mother never told you?" The voice belonged to a satyr in his mid-fifties who had stepped out from behind the vampire Cassius. The short half-man, half-goat, was wearing a pristine three-piece, black suit with a green silk tie. Sitting on his head between his two curved horns was a black bowler hat with a matching green band. His cloven hooves moved swiftly across the green, shag carpet. He was the one whom I had bumped into at the reception.

I stared at the entire group, intently. "Who are you people? How do you know about my mother?" I demanded.

The satyr gestured for all of us to sit down. Once everyone did as he requested, he began to make introductions. "This is Captain Cassius," he said, pointing to the one-eyed vampire. "The two werewolves are General Nessa Wulfsguard, and her brother, Archer." Then he gave me a little bow. "And I am Gunther Hornicus. You got my message and have come to help us."

"I guess so," I said, "but I still have no clue who you are."

"Your Highness, we are your loyal subjects, ready to do your bidding," Gunther insisted with a pleading, persistent look in his brown eyes.

I held up a hand. "Whoa! Whoa!" I said. "Time out! Did you just call me 'Your Highness?' "

"Yes," Cassius said, "you are a princess and the rightful queen of Peregrin."

"Okay, this is a joke, right?" Eddie asked, "because my wife is not royalty."

Wulfsguard immediately conjured up a gun and pointed it

at Eddie's chest with deadly accuracy. "You dare deny her heritage?" she snarled. Her black wolf ears lay flat against her head. "And you, her Guardian?"

"Put the gun away!" I ordered her. "Look, you'd better start explaining what's going on."

Wulfsguard begrudgingly made the gun disappear as Gunther started to speak. "You must come to help us. The queendom is in shambles, and Queen Rachel is an evil tyrant who must be dethroned! She has raised the taxes impossibly high so no one can pay them, the main island has become a haven for criminals who will kill and maim without fear of the consequences, and she has nearly brought famine and drought to the land. We thought Diamondback had killed you, fulfilling her orders, but you're alive!" He paused. "Good people have died because of her."

Diamondback did kill me, but I decided not to address that topic. "You know a Queen Rachel?" I asked hopefully. Finally, someone who could answer all my questions.

"Of course, she is your sister!"

I fervently shook my head. This was getting weirder by the

second. "No! No! No! I don't have a sister!" I searched the minds of Cassius and the two werewolves for any deception, but there was none. They really believed I was their true queen, and they really wanted me to overthrow my sister or whoever she was.

The group looked at me with a look of pure disbelief. "I thought for sure Queen Sara had twin girls," Gunther said.

"No," I said, "You've got me mixed up with someone else."

"No!" Cassius insisted. "Your mother, Queen Sara, gave piano lessons, right?"

My heart caught in my throat. "Yeah," I said in a voice barely above a whisper, "how did you know?"

"She was an exceptional musician, even as a young child," Cassius said wistfully. "We were saddened when she was killed by that drunk driver. We hope to have a remembrance day on April fourth of every year in honor of Queen Sara, with your permission, of course."

A huge lump formed in my throat. The day my mother died. How could they know that?

Eddie looked over at me and grabbed my hand. "You okay, Shelly?"

I managed a nod, but on the inside, I was raging. How dare these strangers play with my emotions by insinuating they knew my mother? "I don't know who you people think you are, but you're sorely mistaken! My mom was never a queen, neither am I, and I don't have a sister!"

"Look," Eddie ordered as he lifted an index finger to the group, "you guys need to back off. You're upsetting my wife."

Gunther seemed to consider his options. "We need your help, but I understand if you refuse to believe us. Ask your father and your stepmother about your mother and sister, and then if you still want to help, come down to the last pier on the left. The Monte Carlo is docked there. We will wait for you, Your Highness."

Chapter Seven:
My Life Turns into a Soap Opera Scene

Eddie and I sat on the idling motorcycle in front of Dad and Amelia's house, a two-story, red raised ranch with a two-door garage. I could see movement behind the lace curtains on the large picture window of the living room. They were still up. "Maybe we should've called first," Eddie suggested as he turned off the bike.

"No," I said. "I want to see their reactions when I ask them."

He looked at me. "Why? Do you actually believe what those people said?"

I hesitated as I stared at the house. "I don't know. They knew all those things about my mom—."

"But, Shell, anyone could have learned those things from

reading her obituary."

"Yeah, but what about me having a sister?"

"I thought you didn't."

"I don't." I rubbed my temples briefly. I was so confused. "I just don't know, Eddie. Which is why I need to ask Dad about this. I'm more inclined to believe him than a group of random strangers."

Eddie blew out a sigh. "Okay, let's go!"

We walked to the maple front door, and I gave it three sharp and loud knocks with the back of my fist. We could hear shuffling, and my dad shouted from inside, "Who is it?"

"It's Shelly and Eddie," I said. "I need to talk to you and Amelia."

The doorknob turned, and my father swung open the door. He narrowed his baby blue eyes at us. "About what?" he asked irritably as he ran his fingers through his short brown hair he always keeps in a military-style cut. "If this is about the wedding—."

I glanced down at the royal blue pajama pants and the matching t-shirt he wore over his six-foot, muscular frame. We had dropped by at an inopportune time, but I wasn't going to let that dissipate my burning questions. "It's not!" I said.

He sighed and beckoned us inside. "This had better be important. Let's go into the living room."

We silently followed him into the living room. Eddie and I sat on the faux leather couch while Dad sat in a blue armchair. There was a moment of awkward silence as I tried to speak but couldn't find the right words. My husband decided to help. "Shelly needs to ask you and Amelia some questions," he said.

"About what?" Dad asked me.

"Timothy!" Amelia called in a seductive voice from upstairs.

"Amelia, we have company!"

My stepmom came down the stairs wearing a long sleeveless red nightgown. Amelia's black hair fell to her shoulders. It amazed me that both of them were in their fifties and had no gray hair. I used to wonder how I would look with gray hair, but now, that doesn't matter anymore. She looked at us with sympathy and surprise in her hazel eyes. "Honey," she asked me, "Are you okay? I know you were only trying to help earlier today."

"This isn't about the wedding," Eddie and I said at the same time.

"Oh! Then why are you here?" she asked.

"A funny thing happened about an hour ago," I said. "A one-eyed vampire, a military general werewolf, her brother, and a satyr in a three-piece suit just told me they knew Mom when she was a little girl. Now they want me to overthrow my twin sister, Rachel, who to my knowledge doesn't exist. All because she's an evil, tyrannical queen."

Both Dad and Amelia gave an audible gasp at the same time. "Cassius and Gunther," Amelia whispered. She looked at my father in shock. "You never told her, Timothy?"

"I promised Sara I would never tell Shelly!" Dad snapped at her. "You could've told Shelly yourself, you know!"

"Told me what?" I demanded.

Dad hesitated. He looked at his wife. "Amelia, you knew Sara's family better than I did."

Amelia looked away from me as tears began to slide down her cheeks. "Your mother was my cousin."

My jaw dropped in shock. "How—No—It can't be!" I glanced over at my father, who turned his head away from me and was nodding his head yes.

"Sara and I are from here."

"Zephyr?" Eddie asked for me.

"Not Zephyr," Amelia said softly, "but a group of isolated islands many miles away. You see, Shelly, your mother was the queen of the land of Peregrin."

"Mom was a queen?" I asked skeptically.

Dad had cupped his head in his hands. "Shelly, just listen to her," he said, refusing to meet my eyes.

"You see," Amelia said, "Peregrin was ruled by a powerful, matriarchal line called Gypsy Mages. These were human women with psychic abilities and were the mediators between the living, dead, and undead. Sara could control people's minds. Each heir to the throne was assigned an undead Guardian to protect them from harm."

"Why do you think I keep referring to Eddie as your 'Guardian,' Shelly?" Dad said.

"I'm not her Guardian," Eddie reminded him. "I'm her

husband. Big difference."

"The Gypsy Mages could also open portals in time and space," Amelia continued as though nothing had happened. "Shelly, Timothy told me how you brought him and Robin here to Zephyr through the purple wormhole."

"No!" I said. "That's not true! I can't open wormholes."

"Yes, you can. You have psychic abilities, Shelly," Dad said. "You can read undead minds, open portals, and have visions. That's extremely rare, even for this world."

"How is this even possible? Mom wasn't from this reality," I protested, still not believing a word that was coming from Dad and Amelia's mouths. "Her parents died in a plane crash."

Amelia shook her head. "No, they didn't. A group of powerful demons overthrew the queendom, and your grandparents were executed. After your mother's sudden coronation, Sara's vampire Guardians, Caleb and Micheline, were instructed to have Sara and I open wormholes to leave this world as soon as possible. We did and came to your world when we were only eight. Caleb and Micheline raised us until high school. Caleb took me to Texas, and Micheline stayed with your mother in Maine."

I searched Dad's face for any falsehood, but there was none. "So, I really am of royal blood?" I asked him.

My father nodded. "Mom told me when we were dating. At first, I didn't believe her until she took me through a wormhole here."

"Wait!" Eddie said. "I thought you had never been here before, Timothy."

"I lied," Dad said reluctantly. "Sara made me promise to never tell anyone about it."

"Even your own children!" I shouted.

"Look, it became even more important after what happened with your sister," Dad said.

"My sister?"

Dad slowly exhaled. "You have a younger twin sister, Shelly. Her name is Rachel."

Shock mixed with anger came over me like a tidal wave as I fell back against the couch. "Then how come I've never met her!" I demanded.

"Because she tried to kill you on several occasions," Dad

said. "After the attempted drowning, Mom called Amelia to ask her to raise Rachel."

"But I failed," Amelia said softly. "After Hank died, Rachel opened a wormhole and ran away right after her fifteenth birthday. I followed her the next day by opening a wormhole myself, but soon lost track of her."

"Well, maybe it would've helped if you hadn't told Rachel about Peregrin," Dad said, bitterly.

"At least it was better than Sara erasing the kids' memories about Rachel," Amelia snapped at Dad.

"We were trying to protect Shelly!"

"Well, your idea of 'protection' sucked," Eddie said, his voice full of quiet rage.

"What do you mean?"

My husband leaned forward on the couch. "The vampire who attacked Shelly is a highly trained assassin. Guess who sent him? Your other daughter."

Dad gasped. "Oh my god!"

"And you did nothing, Dad!" I said. "Did you ever think to mention Rachel to me?"

"It was for your own protection!"

"I almost lost Shelly because of your 'protection,' Timothy!" Eddie shouted.

"We didn't know," Dad said.

"Bull crap!" I shouted angrily. "So meeting Amelia here in Zephyr was another lie. What else have you lied to me about?" I got up from the couch and began pacing back and forth. "Okay, I get the fact that you wouldn't tell me about my evil twin sister when I was a kid. But not even as an adult? And do you know the worst thing about this?" I refused to wait for an answer. "It's that I had to find out about her from a group of strangers." I bolted up from the couch and started to head for the door, but Dad reached out with his elasticity and grabbed my arm.

"Shelly," Dad started to say, "Let us explain—."

I shoved my father's hand away. "No! No more explanation of your lies!" Tears filled my eyes. "I can't even speak to you two right now!"

Dad glanced over at my husband. "Eddie, please reason with her," he pleaded.

Eddie shook his head. "No, Timothy, this is your fault. You

should've told Shelly about her twin sister."

"You've got to understand, Eddie. I was only trying—," Dad started to say, but my husband cut him off.

"Trying what? To get her killed? Because it almost worked!" Eddie snapped at him. My husband used to box, but my dad is a third-degree black belt. I was unsure who would win if a fight broke out.

"Eddie, let's go," I said as I tugged on his arm. I glared at my father and stepmother. "I've got nothing more to say to you!" My husband and I both turned and left the house. I was too angry to say good-bye.

The ride was silent. Eddie wisely left me to my thoughts. I tried to make sense of what I had just learned, but my anger at my parents was too much. How could they lie to me all these years? A sister I never knew. My so-called royal heritage. My mother's ability to pull off a Jedi mind trick. As I mulled the recent events over in my mind, I kept coming back to the same conclusion. I knew what I had to do, but that didn't mean I had to enjoy it. I felt my husband lovingly squeeze my hand.

Once we reached home, he shut off the motorcycle and got off. "So what now?" he asked as he helped me down.

"I'm going!" I took off my helmet and handed it to him.

"To confront your sister?"

I nodded vigorously. "Yes, I need to do this. Maybe, I can talk to Rachel—." I stopped and looked at my husband as he removed his own helmet. "You're not arguing with me?" I asked surprised.

"I think you should definitely go," he answered as he pushed the motorcycle into the shed that he and my father had turned into a garage large enough to fit our two cars, his bike, and Quentin's stable, "but on one condition: I go with you."

"Eddie, this is my fight, and—."

"No, I'm going with you. I'm not going to lose you again." Eddie gave me his winning smile. "We're a team. When we fight, we fight together."

When I read my husband's mind, I found the main reason he wanted to go. Not only did he want to protect me, but he also had a score to settle. "Eddie, what if Diamondback's not there?"

"If he isn't, I will hunt him down."

"And kill him?"

"If it comes to that, yes."

I fell silent. I was determined to confront my sister, and Eddie was determined to kill the man who attacked me. Before the week's end, there was definitely going to be bloodshed, whose I had no idea. I finally let out a sigh. "Well, let's get packing. We have a long journey ahead of us.

Chapter Eight:
Eddie and I Board an Airship

I left a message with my supervisor at the library, telling her a family emergency had come up, and I wouldn't be at work for the next three days. Okay, hunting down my demented sister before she tried to completely put me six-feet under isn't exactly considered a "family emergency," but "death by evil twin" isn't listed as an excused absence in the Zephyr Memorial Library staff handbook.

Eddie's message was a bit more detailed as he told my dad he was going with me to find Rachel but was unsure he would continue working at the diner. I wasn't the only one shocked by my dad's betrayal. Eddie came into the bedroom as I just finished packing our two small rolling suitcases. "What are we going to do with Quentin?" he asked. "I let him in. He's convinced Vinnie has booby-trapped his pen."

Quentin came into the bedroom. "Hey, I have good reason to be paranoid. Vinnie is a psychopath." He spotted our packed bags. "Where are you guys going? Is it on a beach where hot, bikini-clad babes bring you margaritas?" He placed his front claws on the edge of the bed.

"I wish. Talons off the bed!" Eddie ordered him. My husband has a philosophy concerning beds: People belong in beds, not animals, especially enchanted griffins.

"Geesh, take a chill pill," he said as he stuck his beak inside one of the duffle bags and began rooting around our clothes. "No bathing suits?" he asked a touch of disappointment in his tone. "Only basic necessities. You're not taking a vacation, are you?"

I shook my head. "There is a situation we have to deal with."

"Ooh!" The griffin's golden eyes lit up like a kid at Christmas. "Can I help?"

"It's going to be very dangerous," Eddie said.

"I'll provide air support," Quentin suggested.

I hesitated. "I don't know if that's a good idea."

"We'll need all the help we can get to deal with your sister, babe."

"You have a sister? Is she hot?"

"No!" I said sharply. I saw the hurt in the griffin's eyes. "Sorry," I apologized, "it's been a stressful night. All right, we'll take you with us. Just be careful."

A few minutes later, the three of us were driving to the docks in the carrot car. Eddie in the driver's seat, me in the passenger seat, and Quentin and our bags crammed in the back seat. The griffin was sitting hunched up on the back seat, his legs unnaturally tucked under him like a contortionist. "Can you move your seat forward, Shelly?" he whined. "I need some more wing room."

"If I move the seat anymore, my body will meld together," I told him. I was already losing feeling in my feet. I shifted sideways to get more comfortable, but no such luck.

"You know, Quentin," Eddie said, "you wouldn't be this uncomfortable if you had let me use my minimize spell on you."

"Get shrunk to the size of an ant? No, thank you. I don't want any more magic cast on me."

"You would've been shrunk to the size of a puppy."

Quentin decided to turn around for the third time and kicked the back of our seats. He stretched out his body. A tawny wing suddenly covered up the entire front of the car. The car started swerving as my husband strained to see out the windshield.

"Keep your wings to yourself, or I'll clip them!" Eddie warned.

The wing moved out of our way.

Five minutes later, we arrived at the docks, and we all got out, clown-car style. I took a step forward and nearly toppled over. I leaned against the car as the circulation in my legs slowly returned.

Eddie grabbed the bags, and he and Quentin walked over to me. "Okay, where's this Monte Carlo?" my husband asked as he placed a ward on the car.

"Last pier on the—." I stopped mid-sentence as I looked down the row of docks. "Wow!" I breathed.

"Yeah," Eddie agreed. We were staring up at a colossal airship hovering in the air. A gray balloon the length of two football fields and just as high held a gondola shaped like the hull of a huge wooden clipper ship with twelve thick, strong suspension cables at the nose, middle, and tail of the balloon. Two powerful-looking engines, similar to ones on jets, were attached to the stern. The bust of a blue lion had been proudly placed as the ship's figurehead. The words, Monte Carlo, were emblazoned in silver lettering on the starboard side.

"A beautiful ship, isn't she?"

Eddie and I looked up to see Cassius and Gunther standing on the deck. "Yeah," my husband said, "she's amazing."

"You are coming to help us, I take it?" Gunther asked.

"Yes," I said, "and to get some answers."

"Well, then," Cassius said with a huge grin, "Welcome aboard the *Monte Carlo*, your Highness!" He tossed us a wooden ladder over the edge.

Eddie handed our bags to Quentin. "Take our bags and fly up on deck," he told the griffin. "Captain," he called to Cassius, "our griffin's coming up with our bags, and we'll climb the ladder."

The vampire nodded. He watched Quentin as the griffin grabbed the bags' handles with his talons and flew them up on deck. "You've got a very smart griffin, You Highness."

"You don't know the half of it," I mumbled. I began climbing up the ladder as a cold ocean wind swept past me. A few seconds later, Eddie and I were both on deck, and Cassius pulled up the ladder. There was no turning back now.

"Would your Highness like a tour of the *Monte Carlo*?" the captain asked Eddie and me.

"Cassius," Gunther interrupted, "I don't think a tour is pertinent to our situation."

Cassius waved him off. "Nonsense, Gunther, Queen Rachel has been sitting her usurping fanny on the throne for the past ten years, and I don't think an extra hour will change that." He paused and looked at me for confirmation. "Unless her Highness disagrees."

"Oh, no," I said. "We'd love a tour." I glanced around the deck. There was not a door in sight. This was going to be a really short tour.

"Well, come along," the vampire captain said. He fished a walkie-talkie out of his jacket pocket and spoke into it. "I need five teleportation spheres to the main deck, please."

"Coming right up, Captain," said a voice on the other end.

Before Eddie and I could say anything, five rainbow-colored circular objects appeared in front of us. They were about the size and shape of those tacky gazing balls you see on people's lawns. They just hung in the air, suspended by nothing.

"If everyone would touch a ball, the tour shall begin," Cassius instructed.

The second my hands touched the ball, my whole body began to fade in and out as if I were a television channel losing reception. Everyone around us was experiencing the exact same thing. I shut my eyes in panic, and when I opened them again, I found myself in a narrow hall. "Eddie?"

"Right behind you, Shelly," my husband assured me. I glanced behind to see him grinning. "Beam me up, Scotty. That was awesome!"

"I'm okay, too," Quentin said. "Thanks for asking."

Cassius and Gunther were ahead of us. "I must inform the general and her brother that Princess Michelle and her Guardian are here," the satyr said as he excused himself from the group and headed down the opposite way down the hall.

"Now," Cassius said, "there are three levels to the ship. We're on the second level, which is for passengers. We have eight cabins, a dining area, and a conference room. The general and her brother will meet you there when you are ready. Come, let me show you your cabin."

He led us down the hall to the last door on the left and pressed a green, lighted button. The door slid open to reveal a windowless room the size of your standard hotel suite. Two double beds with blue and purple floral bedspreads surrounded one eggshell white metal nightstand with a bolted down lamp, phone, and alarm clock. Everything on the nightstand was bolted down. An eggshell white, wooden table for two and matching chairs had also been bolted down as well. Directly across from the beds was a forty-two inch, plasma flat-screen attached to the blue and purple striped wall.

"The remote in the nightstand drawer will beep if there's an emergency," Cassius explained. "You must turn the television to channel 45 to gain visual access to the navigation room. Another crewmember or I will be able to inform you of the nature of the emergency. You can see and speak with us, but none of the crew will be able to see you." There was also a small closet next to the bathroom.

Eddie took the bags from Quentin and set them by one of the beds. "What about our griffin?" he asked.

"He can stay in the pet holding area on Level Three," Cassius said. He spoke into the walkie-talkie again. "Jake, please come to passenger cabin eight and take the princess' griffin down to the animal hold."

"But—but—but," Quentin started to sputter, but the eye daggers both Eddie and I shot immediately shut him up.

Within seconds, a freckled-face, skinny satyr barely out of his teens appeared in the doorway. He wore a white tank top and tan shorts, which by the irritated look on Cassius' face, I guessed was not the crew uniform for the *Monte Carlo*. "Jake is in the house!" he announced with much flourish before downing the last dredges in his soda can.

"Master Hornicus," Cassius said in a failing attempt to mask the annoyance at his employee, "how many times have I told you to wear your uniform when on duty?"

"It cramps my style, man," Jake said. He expertly tossed the empty can in a nearby trash bin. His lime green eyes studied Eddie and me for a moment. "Wow," he said, nodding his head in approval, "it's an honor to finally meet you, Your Highness! Anything you want or need, Jake's your man. And when you become queen, I would be honored to be a member of the castle staff. I'm a terrific groundskeeper."

Cassius impatiently cleared his throat. "If you are done lollygagging, Master Hornicus, then take the griffin down to the holding pen."

"Oh, sure, man," Jake said. "Come on—what's his name?"

"Quentin," I said.

"Come on, Quentin," the satyr said as he led Quentin down the hall.

Once the two disappeared using the teleportation spheres, the vampire captain smiled at Eddie and me. "Now about that tour?"

The tour was excellent. First, Cassius took us down to the third level or as he referred to "the belly of the ship." This was my husband's second favorite part of the ship. The first stop was the boiler room where we met the Chief Engineer, a gray-skinned, four-foot-tall troll in a blue jumpsuit working on a gigantic boiler. "We should probably fuel up when we land, captain," he informed.

"Good idea," Cassius said.

After giving me a respectful bow, the troll introduced himself as Merkel. Eddie engaged him and Cassius in a discussion about the mechanical aspects of the ship. What the hull was made out of? Carbon fiber. What does the airship run on? Coal. How fast could the *Monte Carlo* go? 85 mph. After that, I zoned out for a while before we continued on the rest of the tour.

We saw the supply room, which was about the size of a walk-in closet, and checked on Quentin in the animal holding area. Then Cassius teleported us up to the top level. "On your left is the sickbay," he said as we walked down another hallway past an open door. I peeked inside. A short, plump vampire dressed in blue scrubs was inspecting the medical supplies in a large cabinet. Her long gray hair was pulled back in a simple braid. "Delilah is the best doctor in the world," Cassius said with a smile, "and I'm not just saying that because she's my wife."

The smell of apple pie drifted by as we walked past a closed door. The captain deeply inhaled. "Ah, Leo must be making dessert in the galley." We walked past several closed doors of the crew's members' cabins. A door slid open behind us, and from the corner of my eye, I saw a chimpanzee leave his cabin and take a teleportation sphere to another part of the ship. I don't know which shocked me more: the four-foot-long bat-like wings protruding from his shoulder blades or the white and blue naval uniform he was wearing. I decided not to say anything.

Cassius led us to the end of the hall and pressed another button. Two large steel doors slid open, and we walked onto the bridge. When Robin and I were in grade school, Dad took us on a tour of a retired battleship somewhere in Virginia. The bridge of the Monte Carlo was very similar to that of the battleship's bridge. A row of various kinds of flight instruments, large interactive computer screens, and tons of blinking buttons and levers lined the wall in front of us. Above them, a large, curved, UV-protected window went halfway around the length of the room.

Sitting at the control panels in swivel chairs were two winged baboons and three Winged Ones (humanoid creatures with angel-like wings.) I glanced over at Eddie. He was like a kid in a candy shop as he took in everything with his dashing green eyes. This was definitely his favorite part of the tour. *I want an airship*, he told me mentally.

I grinned at him. *Think you can build one?* I asked.

No problem.

I walked over and peered out the window at the dark, churning sea passing below us. "When did we take off?" I asked.

"A few minutes ago," Cassius replied. He glanced over the helm to where a gorilla was wearing a uniform similar to the vampire captain's. Every few minutes, the gorilla adjusted a hand lever on his left while effortlessly steering the ship's wheel. "This is Moses Heston, my first mate," the captain said as he clapped a hand on the primate's shoulder.

"We should be arriving in Peregrin in seven hours, captain," Moses said in a gruff voice. A talking gorilla shouldn't have surprised me, having lived in a magical land for over six years, but then again, "surprise" seemed to be the word of the day.

"Very good," Cassius said. "Ladies and gentlemen," he announced to his crew, "this is the true queen of Peregrin, Princess Shelly, and her Guardian, Eddie, who is also her husband!"

"All hail Princess Shelly!" the crew shouted enthusiastically.

"Your reign is very much anticipated, your Highness," Cassius told me. "Shall we adjourn to the conference room? I believe General Wulfsguard and her brother are waiting for you."

I slowly inhaled and looked at Eddie. "Okay, let's go!"

My husband blew out a reluctant sigh. He cast a wistful eye around the navigation room. "Sure," he said.

The captain looked at him. "After the meeting, would you like to take a turn at the helm? If it's okay with the princess."

"Of course, it's okay," I said, reading Eddie's excited thoughts about flying the airship.

Eddie and I followed Cassius out of the navigation room, and once again, we teleported to the second level. The conference room was at the opposite end of the hall, all the way past the passenger cabins. After opening the door, we stepped inside. It reminded me of those war room scenes you see in movies. A large, black oval table sat in the middle of the room with eight black leather swivel chairs surrounding it. The walls were painted battleship gray with no accents or decorations on them.

Wulfsguard was standing up and leaning forward on the table's edge. Her eyes were scanning a large map spread across the entire tabletop. "She has got the entire castle under constant surveillance, Archer. You might be able to hack into the mainframe to shut down the robots.”

“I’ve tried, Wulfsguard,” her brother said, “but Queen Rachel has made the system completely impenetrable.” He got up from his chair and pointed to a specific area on the map. “There might be a small chance of shutting down the robots’ mainframe if we can get inside.”

“Well, we can consider my way,” the general said.

“Ha! The last time we tried that, all of your bombs were disabled.”

Wulfsguard shot her brother a withering glare before both siblings noticed our arrival. “Your Highness,” she said, giving me a respectful bow, “how should we plan our attack?”

The question completely threw me off guard. “Ah—well—.”

Wulfsguard immediately noticed my hesitation. “I assume you have experience,” she said, very matter-of-factly.

I gave a pitiful laugh. Experience. Such a broad term. “Sure,” I lied.

The werewolf narrowed her eyes as if she could see right through my lie. Then again, it was pretty weak. Nevertheless, she decided to give my ideas a shot. "Well, what is your plan?"

"Storm the castle?" I suggested.

"And?" the general asked.

"That's it," I answered.

"Storming the castle has been tried and has failed many times, your Highness," Gunther finally said. He sat at the furthest end of the table, listening quietly.

Eddie raised an eyebrow at me. *Nice plan, MacGyver.*

I shot my husband a not-so-subtle and a very irritated glance. The general, her brother, the captain, and Gunther all looked at me expectantly as if I was some seasoned warrior princess who came up with elaborate battle strategies all the time. These people had really high, unrealistic expectations. "Well, scratch that plan," I said. If I was going to be queen, I had better start instilling more confidence in my loyal subjects by coming up with a workable plan.

I took a long look at the map before us. Wulfsguard had marked every possible access point blocked by my sister's guards. "Okay, tell me about the castle. This is the blueprint, right?"

Gunther nodded. "Castle Delorean was built ten thousand years ago atop Mount Gypsy. The first queen had the castle's exterior built from magical, indestructible bricks and mortar. It is an octagonal shape with a tower at each point. Castle Delorean has five floors, three above ground, and two below ground. The windows have been unbreakable since Delorean was first built.

Each queen has made improvements over the centuries, making the castle practically impregnable. Unfortunately, your sister reconfigured the security system and has replaced all the guards with robots."

"Who shoot plasma weapons," Wulfsguard added.

"Are the former guards still willing to help?" Eddie asked, "because they might know a way in."

"Yes," Gunther confirmed, "the sphinxes will do anything for the royal family."

"Sphinxes?" I asked.

"Yes, eight of them used to guard the castle until your sister nearly killed them with one of her plasma robots," Wulfsguard said in a disgusted voice. "Now those bloody robots patrol the entire perimeter of the castle every fifteen minutes."

"How many robots are there?" Eddie asked.

"One hundred," Archer said.

"And no way to get in without being blasted," Eddie said.

I scanned the map, desperately looking for a way in. A distant memory surfaced to the front of my mind, as I felt a tad dizzy. It was more like a dream. I could see my mother as a little girl playing with her cousin in the tunnels connecting to the castle.

"Shelly?" Eddie asked, touching my arm.

His question brought me back to the present. "Are the tunnels still accessible?" I asked.

Gunther's eyes widened with shock. "The tunnels?" he asked with a cautious edge to his voice.

"Yeah, the three tunnels connected to the fake crypt," I replied, not really knowing what I was saying.

"How do you know about them?" the satyr asked.

"I dreamt about my mom playing in them when she was little."

Gunther and the others exchanged surprised, but elated looks. "The prophecy," he muttered.

"It's been fulfilled," Cassius said.

"What prophecy?" I asked.

Gunther was about to speak, but Wulfsguard interrupted him. "Never mind, Your Highness. Let's hear your plan."

I swallowed. "It looks like one tunnel runs directly to the castle's courtyard."

"Yes," Gunther confirmed, "there is a gardening shed near the koi pond. The tunnel runs directly beneath it."

"Does my sister know about these tunnels?"

"Not to my knowledge, Your Highness," Gunther answered.

"What are you thinking, Shell?" Eddie asked.

"A surprise attack from underground," I answered. I looked at Wulfsguard. "How many people are willing to fight?"

"My lieutenant informed me we have at least 200 men and women, half of those are displaced military personal and are under my command, and the rest are citizens ready to fight alongside their new queen."

No pressure. "Okay," I said, "a handful of us can enter the tunnel while the rest of the army hides just outside the castle walls. When the gates are open, the army can rush in. Would that work, General?"

The werewolf nodded in approval. "Archer and I will accompany you and your Guardian through the tunnel."

"I can open the gates," Archer said.

"I will accompany you as well," Gunther said.

"Okay, we'll attack tomorrow night," I said. "If there's nothing else, I'd say this meeting is adjourned."

We all went our separate ways. While Eddie went to explore the bridge, I went back to the cabin and sat on the edge of the bed, wondering what I was going to do when my stomach began growling. I realized I hadn't really anything eaten since Bruce and Libby's wedding reception. "I wonder if the kitchen's still open."

I left my room and followed my nose to the galley and dining area. Not a soul sat at any of the tables. The kitchen couldn't possibly be closed because I could hear pots and pans clanging and voices coming from the double steel-swinging doors at the rear of the dining area. I chose a table for four and sat down in a black metal chair with hunter green padded backing.

As if sensing my presence, a rectangular-shaped hole opened up in the table, and a ten-inch touch screen flipped up to face me. "High-tech menu," I said to myself. "Nice." Reading over my choices, I selected a grilled cheese sandwich, tomato soup, and a glass of fruit dragon blood. Once I had ordered, the menu disappeared under the table.

"Is this seat taken?"

I looked up to see Gunther standing in front of me. "Not at all," I told him. "Have a seat."

The satyr pulled out the chair across from me. His menu appeared, and he quickly made his selections. "Leo makes an excellent cherry cobbler. I believe he received the recipe from your grandmother." He paused and gave me a curious look. "You're not what I expected for the next queen."

I raised an eyebrow. "Not sure if I should take that as a compliment or an insult."

"Oh, a compliment, your Highness. For one thing, we've never had a queen marry her Guardian."

"Is that a bad thing?"

He shook his head. "Of course not. It's just an uncommon precedent."

"And what's the other thing?"

"A vampire has never been on the throne before."

"Wow! I'm one of a kind then."

"Indeed," he said with a weary smile, and then murmured, "So, the prophecy had foretold."

"You mentioned that at the meeting. What were you talking about?"

A surprised look spread across his face. "Your mother never told you?"

I shook my head. "My parents never told me a lot of things."

"Well, your great-great-great-great-grandmother, Queen Penelope, was given a prophecy by her advisor and the prime minister, the great pamola, Hiram. Now let me see if I can remember the correct words. 'A daughter of the dark shall arise as a queen with the power of a seer. She was once a daughter of the light and will rule both the children of the light and dark for a millennium of peace and prosperity.' The people of Peregrin have been waiting for the prophecy to be fulfilled, and now it has."

I mentally digested that new information while Jake came out from the kitchen carrying our food. "Cherry cobbler and hot chocolate for you, Uncle Gunther," the younger satyr said as he unsteadily balanced the large tray with one hand. "And for the future queen, grilled cheese sandwich, tomato soup, and a tall glass of fruit dragon blood." He set our food down and started to pull up a chair when a tall, slightly overweight minotaur in a cook's uniform pushed his way through the doors. "Jake!" he shouted. "You're not on break just yet. Get back in here!"

"Yes, Leo," Jake said as he scurried back to the kitchen.

"Sorry about my nephew, Your Highness," Gunther said, "He can be impulsive, but he has a good heart."

"Don't worry about it," I told him as I took a spoonful of tomato soup seasoned with rosemary and parmesan. "So, you really believe I've fulfilled this prophecy?"

"Oh, yes, you will be a much better queen than your sister ever will be. Perhaps, the best Peregrin has ever seen."

"Let's just take one thing at a time," I replied. I was honored that this middle-age satyr was confident I could be the greatest queen ever when I wasn't so sure of my own confidence.

"You truly care about people and try to help them when you can." He paused in his praise. "I have a confession to make."

I instantly went on guard. "What?"

"How did you bring your friends, the Millers, to Zephyr?"

"I found a website online on how to open a wormhole and—."

"I created that website, knowing you would find it. You can still open portals in time and space because of your heritage, but you do not need that ridiculous spell I wrote. I didn't mean to deceive you, Your Highness, but when we first heard about how you came to Zephyr, I knew you were the prophesied one."

"But what about my sister?"

He gave a derisive, but sad laugh. "Queen Rachel has neither given the queendom peace or prosperity, and she is not a vampire, unlike you. You must defeat your sister and restore the queendom. It's your duty as the true queen."

I wanted to tell the satyr I was definitely not ruler material, but when I looked into his face, I just couldn't. "I'll try."

"Good."

"Gunther, you seem to know so much about my family."

"My family has served the royals for many generations as the Private Secretary to the Queen. When you succeed in overthrowing Queen Rachel, I would greatly appreciate it if I could retain that position."

That's quite a big "if," I thought to myself. "Uh, sure."

The satyr got up from the table and picked up his tray. "Your Highness, I must warn you about Queen Rachel. She has the power to bring illusions to life."

"Crap," I said under my breath. This was going to be a big problem. I wouldn't know what was real or false.

"I thought it best to warn you and your Guardian."

"Thanks, Gunther."

He smiled and gave a slight bow before leaving the galley. Now that I was alone, I could eat while I thought about my plan to confront my sister. Not that I had much of a plan to begin with. It was more of a germ of an idea. I did know one thing: I wasn't going to kill her. I was a vampire, but not a killer. Maybe I could

reason with her, and we could work out our differences

unscathed. Then again, from what I knew and learned about

Rachel's track record, that was probably not going to happen.

Suddenly I had lost my appetite.

Chapter Nine:
We Take the Scenic Underground Route

The landing announcement over the loudspeakers jarred us awake. Eddie and I shuffled out of bed, showered, and changed into clean clothes. "Cassius said we'll be landing behind the castle at the base of the mountain," my husband said.

"Won't we be spotted?" I asked. My stomach was still doing to flip-flops ever since Gunther told me about my sister's power. I had even worried Eddie when I started dry heaving in the bathroom. I really hoped the bottle of blood I drank would stay down.

"The Monte Carlo has shielding technology. How are you feeling?" he asked as he put on his utility belt.

"Every single one of my nerves is shot, and I still feel like

I'm going to throw up."

"You don't have to do this, Shell."

"Yes, I do. I need to confront Rachel," I said as I slipped on a bulletproof vest over the combat fatigues, which General Wulfsguard insisted Eddie and I wear.

"Okay," Eddie said as he strapped on the combat helmet with the headlamp (another necessity of Wulfsguard's.) "You do know she's going to try to kill you."

"Maybe she won't once we start talking."

"You can't possibly believe that, babe,"

"I know, honey. I was just hopeful," I said as I strapped Knowledge in her sheath onto my back. I slipped on my shield. "You know what? I've been thinking. My shield needs a name."

"It does?"

"Yeah, I've already named my sword."

"Okay, what's the name?"

"I don't know. What do you think?"

Eddie thought for a moment before answering. "How about 'Truth?'"

"I like it, honey. ' Truth' it is."

I remembered my conversation with the satyr and told it to my husband. "Gunther mentioned I'm a seer."

Eddie nodded. "Makes sense, Shelly. Those dreams you've told me about, they've come true."

I nodded, thinking of Dad's story about Rachel attempting to drown me and the corresponding dreams. There were other dreams, ones I would never tell anyone. I began to wonder if those were visions as well.

"That does qualify you as a physic who apparently has fulfilled a major prophecy for these people."

I swallowed hard. Great, I was in the process of fulfilling a prophecy to become this legendary warrior queen. No pressure, right? "I guess so. Let's take down my sister."

We left our room and met with Wulfsguard, Archer, Gunther, and Quentin upon the deck. "Where's Cassius?" I asked as six teleportation spheres appeared in front of us. "The captain and the crew will be staying aboard the ship," Wulfsguard answered just as our molecules played ping-pong with each other as we teleported off the airship.

We materialized on the soft grass in the middle of an eerie cemetery where tombstones rose out of the ground like solemn soldiers of a forgotten age. I looked up at the three full moons hanging in the starry sky. "Wow, beautiful!" I said.

"Yes, Your Highness," said Gunther, "the three moons are lovely. Your grandparents loved to look at them. Well, that was before the Demon Wars," he added sadly. He adjusted the quiver full of strange-looking, purple, and yellow arrows strapped to his back. He hoisted the longbow over his shoulder.

"This way, Your Highness," Wulfsguard said as she beckoned us forward. She took us swiftly and quietly through the cemetery until we reached a large crypt.

A leotaur came rushing at us from behind the seven-foot stone entrance. From the waist up, she was human, but below was a lion's body. She swung a big, energized mace at us with both hands. "Who goes there?" she snarled at us. Her shoulder-length, tawny hair was pulled back into a tight braid under her combat helmet. She wore a black and gray camouflage shirt under her bulletproof vest.

"Lieutenant, halt!" Wulfsguard held up a paw.

The leotaur skidded to stop, but still brandished her mace. "Sorry, general. I thought it was Queen Rachel."

"No matter," the werewolf said. "Your Highness, this is my lieutenant, Astrid Nemean. Lieutenant, this is the true future Queen of Peregrin, Shelly Van Helsing."

"I'm at your command, Your Highness," the lieutenant said with a deep, respectful bow.

"Any word on the enemy's status?" Wulfsguard asked Astrid.

"The triplets should be back from their reconnaissance mission," the leotaur said as she gazed up into the starry night. "They are almost here."

Silhouetted against the three moons, three large owls flew down towards us. As they reached the ground, the birds morphed into three vampires barely out of their twenties. If underwear models combined with godlike beauty, they would look like these guys. All three of them had blond hair, blue eyes, and looked like Fabio on steroids.

"Adonis, Absalom, Arnold!" Nemean ordered. "What is

your report?"

The three vampires spoke as one in an eerie, almost robotic voice. "The entire castle is unaware of the impending attack." Not creepy at all.

"Good," Wulfsguard said. "Let the army know we will attack once the gates have been opened. If that is all right with the princess."

"Sure," I replied, "you're the general."

The triplets stepped towards me in perfect harmony, their long blonde hair flowing behind them. They gave me a respectful bow and then said in complete synchronization, "We wish to become your Guardians."

Eddie stepped forward and put an arm around my shoulder. "Sorry, boys, that position has already been taken." He glanced at me. *As if I'm going to let these robots be your bodyguards,* he told me subliminally.

The three vampires frowned before turning into owls and taking flight. Astrid raced away into the darkness. I looked at Quentin. "Go with them," I told him. "You'll fight better in the air." Quentin gaped open-mouth as if I had just sealed his death sentence. He tried to protest, but one glare from me shut him down. He took flight after the vampire owls.

"Such a strange griffin," the general mused.

"You got that right," I muttered with a shake of my head.

Wulfsguard looked at Archer. "Open the door," she told him.

Eddie and I looked at the crypt and then at each other in puzzlement. The only thing we saw was the words R.I.P. Nirgerep 1384 emblazoned on the cold stone slab. If a door was there, it was cleverly hidden.

Archer placed both palms flat on the crypt's face and shut his eyes. The stone shimmered and seemed to ripple outward under his touch as it began to change shape. Within seconds, Eddie and I realized why the werewolf was given the name Archer. The epitaph was still there, but now it was on the front of a crudely made stone door with a large, iron handle. Archer pulled the door open and beckoned Eddie, Gunther, Wulfsguard, and me to follow him inside.

Once we were inside and flicked on our headlamps, Archer made the door vanish, and we stood cramped in a dark room a little smaller than your standard bank vault. The interior was made entirely of marble and granite. We all stood shoulder-to-shoulder like canned sardines around a large marble sarcophagus with a raised image of a lion serving as its lid.

"So, Archer," I said, breaking the awkward silence, "are you going to create another door?"

"No need to, Your Highness," Archer replied. "The entrance is there." He pointed at the coffin.

"There?" Eddie asked hesitantly. "Inside that sarcophagus?"

"Yes," Gunther replied. "The body inside has been mummified according to—."

"Whoa! Whoa!" I said, holding up my hands. "There is a mummy in there?"

"Yes, is there a problem?"

"Yeah," I said, "my husband and I aren't really huge fans of mummies."

"The last one we encountered tried to kill us," Eddie said.

"It won't come alive, I assure you," Gunther said. He felt around the edge of the sarcophagus with one of his hooves.

"Now, if I remember the stories correctly, there should be a secret lever here somewhere. Ah, ha! Here it is." He pressed down hard on a stone tile, and the floor rumbled beneath us as the coffin lifted upright off the ground.

I peered down the slick marble steps into a pitch-black tunnel entrance. I glanced at my husband. "Here we go!"

"After you, Your Highness," Gunther said to me.

"Okay!" I said, and we all descended into the darkness.

In complete silence, we walked single-file down the corridor. The tunnel ceiling was barely six-feet high and was the same width as an airplane bathroom. Eddie and I led the way with Gunther and the werewolves bringing up the rear. "Oh, crap!" I said softly.

"What is it?" my husband asked.

I read General Wulfsguard's and Archer's minds.

And?

They actually think I have a plan, I said subliminally.

You do have one, don't you? Eddie asked me.

Well, entering the tunnels was as far as my plan went.

"We're so screwed."

"Your Highness?" Gunther asked.

I didn't realize I had said that last thought aloud. "Nothing, Gunther!"

Sudden cries filled the air and stopped us in our tracks. A shudder ran up my spine as the childlike screams died down as quickly as they came. My hand went instantly to the hilt of my sword. "What was that?" I asked.

"Nothing, Your Highness," Gunther assured me, but the hurriedness of his voice betrayed him.

"There are children down here, and they need our help," I said.

"No!" Wulfsguard said.

"I'm the princess, and we will help those children."

Gunther placed a hand on my shoulder. "Your Highness, what we heard were not children."

"What do you mean?" Eddie asked.

"Pookas," Archer said. There was a hint of fear in the werewolf's voice.

"The pookas—," Gunther began to explain, but

Wulfsguard cut him off.

"You can tell her later," the werewolf snapped. "We must get moving."

I took my husband's hand for reassurance. *What's a pooka, Eddie?* I asked him telepathically.

Don't know, but they seem awfully scared of them. "Are we in danger?" my husband asked the satyr and the two werewolves.

"No," Wulfsguard said, "the pookas are in the tunnels on either side of us. The walls haven't been breached yet. Come, and no more talking."

We stopped in our tracks. Eddie lifted up his flashlight to reveal an old, rusted, metal rung attached to the mountain's stonewall. "Wow!" he breathed, "that's a good three hundred-foot climb."

"Yes," Gunther said, "there are seven more of these."

"This is the only way up there?" I assumed.

"Yes, Your Highness," Wulfsguard said.

I gave an exaggerated sigh. "All right." I watched as my husband began to scale the rungs, hoping they would hold his weight. How many years ago did Gunther say this tunnel was built? I took a deep breath and began to climb. The rust left reddish stains on my palms as I carefully ascended the ladder. About halfway, a rung crumbled beneath my right foot. I let out a gasp of terror as I started to slip.

Eddie's arm shot out and grabbed my wrist before I plummeted. Being an immortal vampire, I wouldn't have died from the fall but would've been in tremendous pain. "Gotcha!"

"Thanks," I breathed.

"Careful, that last step's a doozy."

I smiled despite the scare. "Onward and upward." I would like to tell you I didn't fall or stumble through the rest of the mountain tunnel, but I would be lying. I fell three more times on the first ladder and at least five times on each of the other seven ladders. Fortunately, Eddie was always there to catch me.

We finally reached the end of our dangerous journey. Archer created another door, and we emerged from the tunnel into a gardening shed, which had been converted into a small armory. The walls were lined with plasma and vaporizer guns of all shapes and sizes. Archer selected a bazooka-shaped weapon I recognized as a plasma firearm. He hoisted the gun on his shoulder and opened the door. "Let's go."

"No, let me flush them out first," Wulfsguard ordered. She conjured up two hand grenades and pulled both pins out with her teeth. "Everyone take cover!" she shouted to us as she lobbed both weapons through the open door.

Nobody hesitated. Just as we hit the ground, two simultaneously loud KABOOMs went off. Our cover was totally blown. Eddie got up and grabbed a blue and silver, shotgun-size vaporizer off the wall. He set the sci-fi-like weapon to its highest setting: Kill.

I looked at my husband. "You already have two guns. Why do you need another one?"

"Because this one's bigger with more firing power," Eddie said.

"You just want a vaporizer."

"Of course, Shelly. I've always wanted one."

"Whatever," I said with a smile. I looked at my so-called subjects as I activated my shield. "Let's take down my sister!" I said, drawing my sword.

We rushed out from the shed, straight into the firing line of five robots. "Move! Move! Move!" I ordered. We dropped to our knees just as a plasma blast from a robot incinerated the shed.

Gunther dropped to his knees. He expertly drew an arrow from the quiver on his back and placed it on the string of his bow. He reached into his pants pockets and took out a small silver lighter with the words "From E. B. with love." He flicked the top with his thumb, and a flame hovered over the lighter. The satyr lit the tip of the arrow and extinguished the fire.

After slipping the lighter back into his pocket, he drew the bolt back and released it. With deadly accuracy, the arrow landed in the second robot's forehead. When it hit the robot, a ball of fire the size of a school bus erupted and cremated the other robots.

Eddie and I looked at the middle-aged satyr in shock. "What was on that arrow tip?" I asked.

Gunther smiled. "Highly concreted nitroglycerin."

"Do you freelance as the Green Arrow?" I asked.

"Enough talking!" Wulfsguard shouted. "We need to get inside the castle." We ran for the twenty-foot, oak double doors with reinforced iron bars. "Archer, get those doors open," she said as she fired at two more charging robots.

The second her brother placed his palms on the doors, an electrical shock knocked him to the ground. I bent down and felt around the werewolf's neck for a pulse. "He's breathing, but unconscious," I said.

"Wench!" Wulfsguard growled as she looked back at the castle where two shadowy figures stood on a large balcony. I realized the general was referring to my sister. Wulfsguard took aim at the balcony with her laser gun.

The woman came out of the shadows and clapped her hands together. A giant ball of ice flew down at Wulfsguard, encasing the gun and her hands in ice.

"Your Highness," Gunther said as he began to perform first aid on the unconscious Archer, "you and your Guardian must get inside and stop Queen Rachel and Diamondback."

"Any ideas?" I asked.

Gunther opened his mouth to say something but stopped

when he looked up in the sky. Eddie and I followed his gaze and gasped in horror. A flying dinosaur with the wingspan bigger than a bus zoomed toward us. It had a long, thin neck with a bulbous shape on its long, pointed beak. "Quetzalcoatlus," I breathed as I gripped Knowledge tightly.

"What?" Eddie asked.

"Quetzalcoatlus," I said, "the biggest flying dinosaur ever to exist." I pressed my back against the doors.

"I'm guessing it's not a herbivore."

"Good guess."

"Super!" Eddie aimed the vaporizer at the living fossil and fired, clipping one of the wings. With a painful screech, the quetzalcoatlus fell to the ground about ten feet from us. It flopped around like a wounded bird before uprighting itself and began walking on all fours like a bat. A giant bat from the seventh layer of Hell. The flying reptile's long neck shot forward, snatched the vaporizer from my husband's hands, and snapped the gun in two with its long, but mighty beak. Eddie stepped in front of me, shielding me from the creature. "Now what?" he asked.

"Not get eaten by a quetzalcoatlus?" I suggested.

"I know this has nothing to do with our situation, but how do you know that name?"

"My mom had me and Robin write a paper on a dinosaur. I chose the quetzalcoatlus. Never thought one would try to eat me, though."

"Nebulae!" Eddie snarled at the creature. Two giant balls of white, scorching fire flew from his open palms. Unfortunately, his fire spell had the same effect as a burn from a curling iron. "Any brilliant ideas, Shell?"

"None. I'm drawing a blank."

"We're screwed."

"Yep."

Lady Luck must have smiled upon us because four-winged creatures swooped down upon the reptile. Each one had the head of a jackal, a lion's body, falcon wings, and a python's tail. I had seen pictures of them and recognized them immediately. The two larger sphinxes were horse-size, and the other two were the same size as a Great Dane. They landed on the flying dinosaur and began to viciously attack it. Eddie and I watched the sphinxes strip the quetzalcoatlus to a fossil-like state.

"Anubis, Set, get those doors opened for the princess and her Guardian!" the largest of the sphinxes, a male with a coat as white as fresh snow, ordered the smaller ones. "Apophis and I will watch your backs."

"Move, your Highness," the gray sphinx ordered us with the voice of a teenager. He and the red sphinx rushed to the closed doors. "Now, Set!" he ordered.

"Got it!" the red one called Set said. They got on either side of the doors and flung their tails at it. The doors splintered with a loud CRACK! Two more whacks with their powerful tails knocked the doors off their hinges.

"Go! Go!" Anubis ordered me.

Eddie grabbed my hand, and we raced through the open doors. We found ourselves in a hall the size of a football field. Several doors lined both sides of the hallway. At the end were two elegant, double staircases made of white and gold painted wood that wound up three levels.

On the first stairway balcony stood the woman I had seen in my dreams. She was about my height with long, light brown hair like my mother and dark eyes. What really made me gasp was the vampire standing next to her. His yellow eyes seemed to bore into me. "Get rid of them!" she ordered Diamondback. She turned and began to run up the stairs.

Diamondback leaped over the staircase and began running at us. I hesitated and looked at Eddie. I wanted to follow my twin, but I also wanted to stay with my husband and fight Diamondback. I had to make a choice.

"Go after her, Shelly," Eddie said.

"Are you sure?" I asked him.

"Yes."

I could clearly read the determination in his green eyes. "Be careful." I raced up the stairs, only pausing for a moment to glance over my shoulder. *I love you, Eddie*, I said telepathically. *I love you, too, Shelly*, Eddie said. He turned his gaze upon the fast approaching vampire. "You're mine, Diamondback."

Chapter Ten:
Battle Between the Guardians

Disclaimer: I've asked the one person who was there to tell what happened next in his own words. Why? For one thing, I wasn't there, and two, he did such a great job telling me later. So, I'll step aside and let Eddie tell you about the battle between the Guardians.

I watched my wife sprint up the stairs after her sister, taking two steps at a time. I wasn't the only one keeping an eye on Shelly. Diamondback's cruel eyes focused on her and readied himself to jump her. It wasn't the first time I had seen him in that attack position. Those long-ago memories of that night resurfaced. I never had entirely told Shelly about my first encounter with Diamondback. I hadn't told her how he brutally killed two members of my team by beating them until they couldn't fight back and then slowly twisting their heads off. When beaten senseless, even the oldest and mosts experienced vampires need hours and sometimes days to completely heal. To this day, I still don't know how I survived the massacre.

The rage inside me exploded. "Duracell!" I snarled. I sent two giant beach ball size, blue energy spheres hurling towards Diamondback.

The energy sent the assassin slamming into a nearby door, cracking it in two. The vampire's body disappeared into the room. I raced in after him, not caring that the spell had drained my own energy. The room was large and dark as my eyes searched for a thermal heat outline of Diamondback. I groped around for a light switch, wondering if Shelly's ancestors had ever installed electricity. Something hit me, and I heard the back of my left knee pop. I crumbled to the floor in agonizing pain.

"I remember you," Diamondback sneered as he kicked me in the ribs. "Operation Wrangler? That was the name of your mission, right?"

I clenched my teeth and tried not to inhale too hard. The son of a hellhound had broken a couple of my ribs. I lifted up a hand and snarled, "Nebulae!" The white fireball flew from my open palm at the vampire's black duster.

He laughed as my fire spell disintegrated on his coat. "You pitiful excuse for a vampire! I'm fireproof."

I rolled onto my back and kicked him below the belt with my good leg. He staggered back in surprise, but not in pain. Crap, he even had protection down there, but at least, it gave me an extra few moments to retrieve a wooden stake from my Batman belt. When he was in range, I lunged up and drove the stake as hard as I could into his heart. The wood splintered apart.

Diamondback smiled maliciously as he saw the horrified shock registering on my face. "The body armor belonged to one of your teammates. Sampson, I believe his name was."

Bile crept up in my throat. Sampson Lestat. A headstrong rookie, but a good kid. He and his wife, Annabelle, another member of my team, had just celebrated their third anniversary when we went on the mission. When the Agency's medical examiner performed Annabelle's autopsy, I found out she was two months pregnant. "You sick maggot," I said through clenched teeth.

"I am indestructible. Nothing can touch me!"

No more magic, just brawn. Kneeling painfully, I sucker punched Diamondback in the throat and then gave him a powerful uppercut to his jaw. This time, the assassin did stagger back in surprise. He obviously never boxed.

I pushed my body up against the wall and took a semi-fighting stance. Pain shot through me the moment I put pressure on my injured knee, and I nearly blacked out. Come on, Eddie, I told myself. You've got to make it out of here alive. Shelly needs you.

I recalled my conversation with Cassius. I was the first Guardian to marry my Royal Charge. My role as a Guardian was mainly a bodyguard to protect and defend my Royal Charge with my life. I remembered what Cassius told me as I piloted the Monte Carlo, "You love the princess very much, and I know you'll protect her with your life. I've seen Guardians come and go, but you're going to be the best one the royal family will ever have."

Diamondback recovered quickly and came back running at me. He jumped and drove his boot into my already injured knee. The sudden burst of intense pain brought me back to reality. As I crumpled to the floor, the last thing I saw was the sole of a boot coming straight at my face before my world fell into darkness.

When I came to, I was still lying on my side on the floor and in intense pain. Only a few things had changed. Flickering candlelight caused dancing shadows along the walls. After finally forcing my eyes open, I could see vague outlines of battle axes, spears, swords, and shields. I tried to move, but something was confining me. I looked down and realized I was wrapped up in something gray and sticky. I knew now how bugs caught in a spider web felt.

"Do you like my new body?" Diamondback asked. I forced my eyes to focus on my attacker or whatever he had changed into. He looked the same from the torso up, but the rest of him was a man-size, black spider. "Oh, yes, one of my last victims was a talented wizard who granted me the power to change into this beautiful body. Actually, his blood gave me power. I just wanted to show you my new body before I killed you, Van Helsing." He had searched me for identification and had found my wallet. "Your wife will definitely see it before she dies."

I breathed a momentarily sigh of relief. Shelly was okay for now, but I needed to stop him. There was one thing I hadn't told my wife: the real reason I was late the night she was turned.

A screaming match had broken out at the diner between a woman and Kim, one of the servers. She had complained about her food being too cold and refused to listen to reason. I was working in the kitchen when I was called out front. As the diner's night manager, I went out to calm the situation down. The customer called Kim a very unkind name and threw a punch at her, fortunately missing her. "Look," I told the woman, "if you don't leave the premises, I'm going to call the police." She took my suggestion and left, but not before shooting a knowing smile.

After seeing Shelly's sister on the stairs, I realized Rachel was that angry customer. The whole fight was a diversion to prevent me from saving my wife from Diamondback's attack. I wasn't going to let him hurt her again.

Rage and survival-fueled adrenaline filled me as I concentrated on turning my body into mist. Once I was in mist form, I drifted out of my sticky prison with all my strength and reappeared on my knees. I was reaching for my utility belt when I saw it halfway across the room. It was useless. The scumbag had torn it off. I was too weak to do any magic and was too weak to fight back with my fists. *I need a weapon, now*, I told myself. What would my MacGyver do? She would turn something into a weapon, whether it was a can opener or a fire extinguisher.

I glanced at a painting on the floor next to me. A farmer was harvesting his crops with a scythe. But what was wrong with the picture caught my eye. For one thing, the scythe's handle was silver and had a ring of sapphires near the top. The second thing, the blade was at a ninety-degree angle, making harvest difficult. Also, the images in the painting were moving.

In my time at Urbana College of Magic, I remembered a course on magically concealing essential items in paintings. I really hadn't paid attention to how objects could be hidden because I was focused on the cute girl two seats in front of me. Not my fault. Listening to the professor was about as exciting as watching grass grow. The only thing I remember from that class was how to retrieve something from a painting. All you had to do was reach into the artwork and pull out whatever you had stored there. Simple really. That was the only thing I had gotten right on the final exam.

I reached into the painting and grabbed the scythe from the farmer's hands. When I pulled it out, it became a six-foot-tall weapon with a two-foot-long, sharp blade.

Diamondback's yellow eyes (Shelly was right, they did have red flecks in them) focused on my newly acquired weapon. His face hardened. "Give it to me, and I'll make your death less painful. Only the king can have the royal scythe, and you're not worthy of that. That honor belongs to me when I marry Queen Rachel and take the throne."

It was then that I realized I had to end this now. There was no chance in Hell I would ever let this monster rule anybody. He had killed innocent people. With the power of a king, he would kill even more, and no one would stop him. "You can have this scythe when you pry it from my cold, dead fingers," I said, even though my jaw hurt beyond belief. It was probably broken, but slowly healing via my vampire abilities. How long was I out?

I swung the war scythe in a sideways arc and took out two of the vampire's spider legs. "That was for all those innocents you've slaughtered," I said as Diamondback stumbled forward. "And this is for my wife." I lifted up the scythe once again and brought it down upon the back of the assassin's neck with all my remaining strength. The blade effortlessly sliced clean through bone and muscle. The head dropped to the floor with a wet thump. The rest of his body teetered for only a few seconds before collapsing.

My breath came in ragged, painful gulps of air as I watched and waited for any sign of movement from the beheaded Diamondback. How many of my ribs did the scumbag break? When he didn't move, I used the war scythe to pull myself to my feet, but not before I grabbed the nasty vampire's head by his long, bone-white hair and looked into the vacant eyes staring back at me. "I guess you're not decapitation-proof."

Swinging the dripping head over my shoulder and using my new weapon as support, I hobbled out of the room with fresh, intense pain accompanying every one of my movements. When I got to the bottom of the stairs, I listened for any signs of my wife, hoping against hope that she was still alive.

"Is that all you've got, Rachel?" I heard Shelly shout from somewhere on the next floor.

I managed a smile. Shelly was still alive and fighting, as far as I could tell. Hopefully, a lot better than I fared, but she still needed my help. I gathered up what little strength I had left and made the arduous and incredibly painful journey up the stairs.

Chapter Eleven:
A Really Bad Case of Sibling Rivalry

I watched as my husband hurled two powerful energy

spells at Diamondback. I wanted to stay and fight, but I had to

confront Rachel. Eddie can take care of himself. He'll be okay, I

told myself. Taking the stairs two at a time, I chased my sister up

to the second level. I wanted to call out her name but decided

against that move in case she tried to kill me again. I followed

her into a massive room with no door. I immediately realized we

were in what used to be a giant library the size of a hockey rink,

but the cobweb-laced shelves were devoid of books, and the

walls were empty of knowledge. I needed to concentrate on

finding my sister. Where was she?

The sound of a chainsaw echoed throughout the room. A figure stepped out of the shadows in the back of the unused library. He wore an apron made of human flesh over his white short-sleeve shirt, tie, and trousers, but the mask made of human skin really got my attention. "Leatherface? You've got to be kidding me!"

The horror movie villain raised his bloodied chainsaw high over his head as he ran towards me. His cowboy boots echoed loudly on the marble floor, but he seemed surprised I didn't run in the opposite direction, screaming like a little girl. He was even more shocked when I delivered a powerful roundhouse kick (a little thing I had learned from my third degree, black belt father) to his sternum, cracking it in two. The live chainsaw clattered to the ground, and I kicked it away from him, taking care not to slice off my foot in the process. Take that, Leatherface. When he realized his weapon was out of reach, he pulled out the butcher knife hanging off his belt.

"Really?" I said. "You're going to bring a butcher knife to a swordfight? Let's see how well that turns out." This fight wasn't going to last long. He lunged at me, preparing to drive the knife into my heart, but Knowledge was much faster. Leatherface staggered back in shock, clutching his bleeding abdomen, and then he vanished before my eyes, chainsaw, and all.

It suddenly dawned on me. If Rachel could make illusions come to life, then she could definitely take them away. Maybe the robots were all just illusions and controlled by Rachel's mind. I spotted my sister huddled in a corner, cupping her head as if she were in pain.

A germ of an idea slowly budded in my brain. Once one of Rachel's illusions was killed or disassembled, it hurt her to the point of making the creation disappear. I started to walk towards her but didn't get very far because three more horror movie villains appeared in front of her. Freddy Krueger, Jason Voorhees, and Michael Meyers. My psychotic sister was sending a whole slew of slasher movie villains to kill me off, and I still had no idea why I was her target.

Freddy was quickly dispatched with a quick stab to the heart. His image flickered a couple times before snapping out of existence. Rachel's face contorted in pain. Now I could concentrate on Jason and Michael, and believe me, killing them wasn't going to be easy.

I had never seen Halloween or Friday the 13th, and I was at a loss on how to kill them. According to my brother, one of them was immortal. I was so lost in my thoughts that I nearly missed the blade of Jason's machete about to gouge out my eyes. I took a couple of quick steps back and kicked the knife out of his hand. Deactivating my shield, I gripped Knowledge with both hands and swung it in a wide arc at Jason and Michael. Seconds later, their heads rolled off their bodies, and they faded out of existence.

"Why are you trying to kill me, Rachel?" I demanded.

My sister got up from her hiding place and stepped into view. She wore a white, form-fitting shirt with black leather pants, black leather jacket, and expensive three-inch stiletto heels. I don't know how she managed to walk comfortably in her outlandish outfit. She must have spent a fortune on shoes alone. "Because of what you did!" she said with a snarl, distorting her beautiful face.

"What I did? What are you talking about? What have I ever done to you?"

Suddenly, two sais appeared in her hands. Even though the three prong dagger-like weapons were intimidating, the middle prongs were even more deadly. Instead of a straight point, the middle prongs were curved to inflict maximum pain and damage. Rachel broke into a run, and the fight was on. One of her weapons sliced my forearm before I had time to activate Truth. I gave a quick jab with Knowledge, but she blocked it with her sai. I kicked out at her legs, but she leaped in the air and gave my shield a hard kick. I stumbled backward but quickly regained my footing.

"You were always the favorite daughter! Mom and Dad loved you more!"

"What are you talking about?" I jabbed my sword again and again, but she blocked my every move.

"I was able to open wormholes when I was four, but when I told Mom, she stifled my potential. But not you. She encouraged you in everything you did. You were the special one."

"That's not true! Mom and Dad would never pick favorites among their kids!"

"Oh, please, Shelly, don't be so naïve! Mom told us we were destined to be queens. Of course, I should have been born first. I'm stronger and smarter than you will ever be! I tried to show them that, but they just said I was a troubled child. You kept tattling on me, telling Mom and Dad how naughty I was."

"You shoved me down the stairs three times, pushed me in front of moving traffic, and tried to drown me. Yeah, I'd call that naughty!" I said. She kicked at my legs again, and I lost my balance. I did a backward flip (something I could've never accomplished when I was human) and was back on my feet.

She barely missed my abdomen with her sai as she continued with her angry monologue. "But you know what? Mom and Dad didn't love me. Instead of helping me, they sent me away to that wench Amelia and her lecherous husband, Hank, when I was only seven. When Mom died, Dad didn't allow me to come to her funeral."

I tried to speak, but the news rendered me speechless. I was shocked. I understood Dad was protecting me from Rachel's violent tendencies, but still, he should've let her come to our mother's funeral. Our parents should have done a lot of things differently. I looked into my estranged sister's eyes and saw nothing but years of resentment and violent rage. Perhaps she was happy at one point in her life, but now her soul was tainted with jealousy and hate. "I'm so sorry," I said sincerely.

Rachel smirked as she read the shock on my face. "That's your problem, Shelly. You've always been weak. Which is why you'll never be queen."

"Empathy and sympathy are not weaknesses. It's what makes us human."

"You're not human anymore."

"Humanity is not what you are, it's who you are."

Her response was a violent head butt.

That was going to leave a mark. I needed to reason with her before one of us got killed. "I don't want to hurt you, Rachel. We can talk about this."

"I don't want to talk!" She screamed at the top of her lungs. "I want you dead."

Okay, that was unproductive. I tried another angle. "Don't blame me for Mom and Dad's actions. I had nothing to do with it."

She jabbed me again in my sword arm with one of her weapons, drawing blood. Out of instinct, I lost my grip on Knowledge and began to put pressure on the wound. Rachel made her sais disappear, and she grabbed for my sword, but I kicked it well out of her reach.

Rachel's eyes filled with rage as she clapped her hands together. "Good-bye, dear sister!"

A massive wall of water came rushing at me. No way was she going to try to drown me again. I leaped to the top shelf of a bookcase for safety. The water was only a few feet below my perch. "Is that all you've got, Rachel?"

She gave me an evil smile as she made the water vanish. "You're hard to kill, but I will find your weak point." She conjured up a spear made entirely out of wood and threw it at me. Good thing her aim was off by a few inches because the spear hit the wall right below my armpit. I leaped off the bookcase and landed on the soaked wooden floor.

Another wooden spear appeared in my evil twin's hands. She was about to throw it at me when I heard a familiar voice say, "I found your Guardian!"

I looked at the doorway and saw my husband leaning heavily on a golden scythe with a blade at a ninety-degree angle. He didn't look good at all. The right side of his face was black and blue, his right knee was twisted and swollen, and each time he took a breath, he winced in extreme pain. He managed to throw a bloody round object into the room before stepping inside and collapsing against the wall in sheer exhaustion.

Rachel screamed in anguish as Diamondback's head rolled to her feet. "You killed Enzo!" Eddie had killed her lover.

A distant memory resurfaced to the front of my mind. A little boy and his two sisters are playing outside. A black cat saunters over to one of the girls and begins to rub itself against her leg. The girl screams in fear and runs back inside.

I switched back to the present and saw my sister looming over my injured husband with a long sword in her hands. She prepared to bring the blade down when I called her. "Still afraid of cats, Rachel?"

She stopped in mid-swing and turned to me. The air around me shimmered in swirling black and gold colors. I dropped to my knees, but barely felt the change in my body.

Holy crap, Shelly! Eddie's telepathic message was full of amazement. *You can turn into a black panther!*

Seconds later, I took a running leap as my new animal body let out an animalistic scream. Claws extended, I lashed at my sister's face, leaving superficial, but bloody marks across her left cheek and knocked her away from my husband. I paced back and forth as a barrier between Rachel and Eddie. I snarled at my sister, daring her to come forward.

She slowly began to back away from me. I could smell the fear coming off her in waves. Then she opened a wormhole off to her right and jumped in.

I should have followed her, but I didn't. Chasing Rachel could wait, tending to Eddie's injuries was more critical. I forced myself to change back into my vampire body (fully clothed, thank God.) I knelt down beside my husband. "How are you feeling?"

"I'm in incredible pain!" He managed a weak smile. "Great vampiric shapeshifting back there! No wonder you can be so wild in the bedroom."

I shook my head at him. "Okay, where is the pain located, honey?"

He winced in pain. "Diamondback broke my jaw and broke some of my ribs after he kicked me in the back of the knee, twice."

"You took care of him, though," I said. I noticed the war scythe he was clutching in his hands. "Where did you find that?"

"Pulled it out of a painting."

"Really?"

He nodded as he winced in pain. "Diamondback had beaten me up pretty badly by then, and I realized the painting served as a hiding place for objects. I took him out with the war scythe."

I looked at him. "You're in a lot of pain. We need to get you to a doctor."

"Shelly, I'm a vampire. I'll heal on my own."

"Yes, you can, dear, but you're going to a doctor. That's final."

He sighed in defeat.

We heard the sound of hooves running up the stairs.

"Your Highness? Mr. Van Helsing?"

"In here, Gunther."

The satyr ran into the room. "Oh my god!" he said, surveying the scene in front of him. "Where is Queen Rachel?"

"Gone," I said. "She disappeared into one of her wormholes. I don't know where."

"And Diamondback?"

"Dead," Eddie said flatly.

Gunther gave a big sigh of relief. A burden seemed to lift off his shoulders. "I have a battle report. The robots have all disappeared. We have no casualties. Delilah is taking care of Archer and the general. "Is your Guardian okay, Your Highness?"

"Yeah, but he'll need to have Delilah look at him and get some kind of fruit juice in him."

"Wouldn't blood be better for him?"

"No," I said, "Eddie's allergic to blood."

"Juice will be fine," Eddie said.

Gunther thought for a moment. "I believe we have some orange juice in the kitchen. I'll bring back some men to help your Guardian." He ran out of the room.

"No pulp in the juice!" Eddie called after the satyr, who stopped and looked back.

"Don't listen to him, Gunther! Whatever you have will be fine!" I shouted. I shot my husband an irritated look. "No pulp? Seriously, Eddie?"

Two nights later, Eddie and I were lying in bed back in our Zephyr apartment. I had told the people of Peregrin I would make my decision tomorrow. We hadn't told anyone in Zephyr about what happened with Rachel. My husband was still healing from the attack. His knee would be out of its cast in the next two days, and his ribs were still a little sore. We were weighing the pros and cons of me taking the throne of Peregrin. "Well, if you did accept the throne, we would have our own house and not have to worry about eviction," Eddie pointed out as he adjusted his leg to get it more comfortable. "Albeit, the house will be a huge castle."

"Yeah, that's true," I said.

"And our financial problems would be solved."

"True as well, but—."

He heard the hesitation in my voice. "What's the matter, Shelly?"

"I have no management experience. I don't feel qualified to rule over a country."

"Shelly, you've got great leadership skills. When we had to get rid of that book demon, you put together a plan and gave the people specific duties to pull it off. You did the same thing with the zombies. People look up to you as a leader, even me. And I'm not saying that because you're my wife."

I smiled. "I have to think about this. It's a huge, life-altering decision. What do you think I should do?"

Eddie put his arm around me. "It's your decision, babe. Whatever you choose, I'll fully support you."

We were silent for a long time as I thought about this decision. Whatever choice I made, I couldn't go back on it. That wouldn't be fair to anyone. Finally, I made up my mind and told my husband my decision.

He kissed me on the lips. "You're making the right choice, Shelly."

I nodded. "You're right, and I feel at peace about it," I replied before turning off the bedside lamp.

COMING SOON

Quests of the Undead

My Life Among the Undead:

Book 9

By
Camara M. Bragdon

Shelly Van Helsing has a new job as the vampire queen of Peregrin, and it isn't eating chocolates and bonbons every day, although she wishes it were. When she and her vampire husband, Eddie, find out that the prime minister, Hiram the Pamola, was accused of stealing the seven firestones, the queendom's source of wealth, they go to confront him. They discover Hiram has been imprisoned by his thieving, despicable brother, Laban. The only way Shelly and Eddie can rescue the prime minister is by bringing back the hidden firestones to Laban, and Hiram will be released. With the help of some new friends, the Van Helsings must take on seven dangerous and deadly quests. Will they survive, or will the reign of Queen Shelly and King Eddie be a short-lived one?

ABOUT THE AUTHOR

Camara M. Bragdon has since escaped the snowy tundra of Maine and now lives in sunny southwest Florida with her cat. Mistoffelees. When she is not writing, she brings joy and learning as a children's and teen librarian, taking pictures and telling terrible puns.This is her eighth book in the *My Life Among the Undead* series, Visit her website at http://camarambragdonauthor.com